FOURTH DOWN AND OUT

## ANDY HAYES MYSTERIES

by Andrew Welsh-Huggins

*Fourth Down and Out*

*Slow Burn* (forthcoming)

# FOURTH DOWN AND OUT

AN ANDY HAYES MYSTERY

## ANDREW WELSH-HUGGINS

SWALLOW PRESS
OHIO UNIVERSITY PRESS
ATHENS

Swallow Press
An imprint of Ohio University Press, Athens, Ohio 45701
www.ohioswallow.com

Printed in the United States of America
Swallow Press / Ohio University Press books are printed on acid-free paper ⊗ ™

First paperback printing in 2015
ISBN 978-0-8040-1153-2

24 23 22 21 20 19 18 17 16 15    5 4 3 2 1

Library of Congress Cataloging-in-Publication Data
Welsh-Huggins, Andrew.
Fourth Down and Out : an Andy Hayes mystery / Andrew Welsh-Huggins.
    pages cm. — (Andy Hayes Mysteries)
    ISBN 978-0-8040-1152-5 (hardback) — ISBN 978-0-8040-4059-4 (pdf )
    1. Private investigators—Ohio—Fiction. 2. Ex-football players—Fiction. 3.
Columbus (Ohio)—Fiction. 4. Mystery fiction. I. Title.
PS3623.E4824F68 2014
813'.6—dc23
                        2014000940

# To Mary Anne Huggins

*For your love, support, and willingness to*

*overlook all those overdue library book fines*

"I am quite used to being beaten and having things thrown at me."

—Odysseus, in Homer's *Odyssey*

Columbus is a town in which almost anything is likely to happen and in which almost everything has.

—James Thurber, *My Life and Hard Times*

# 1

"HEY! WOODY HAYES!"

I was almost home when I heard the man's voice. I shouldn't have turned around. Partly because I haven't been called that name by anyone I consider a friend in close to two decades. And partly because events earlier in the evening should have alerted me to trouble.

But turn around I did, and that's when he hit me full in the face. With the flash of a cell phone camera.

"Woody Hayes," the man repeated. "I don't believe it."

I stepped back, eyes adjusting in the dark to the flash, and made out a man in a ski mask a few feet in front of me holding a phone in one hand and something I couldn't quite make out in the other.

"What the hell?" I said, and instinctively raised the baseball bat I keep in my van and had carried with me on the short walk to my house just in case. Because of what happened earlier. Which shows what a doofus I was to turn around in the first place.

That's when I saw the shotgun.

"Laptop," he said. "Nice and easy and no one gets hurt."

"What if I say no?"

"What if I blow you away and just take it?"

"Why do you want it?"

"Why don't you shut the fuck up?"

I debated my options. I didn't want to give up the laptop. But I knew better than to try something dumb like pitting my bat against his gun.

"All right," I said. "It's all yours."

"Set it down," he said, gesturing with the gun. "And the bat too."

I followed his instructions. I lowered the cardboard box holding the computer onto the narrow, brick-paved street, then set the bat beside it.

"Now turn around and get lost."

"Still curious why you want it," I said.

"Move it."

So I turned around, slowly, and started walking. I hadn't made it more than ten feet when I heard the sound of boots on brick, turned back, and was just in time to raise my arms and deflect a blow from my own baseball bat that appeared to be destined for my head. I staggered back, forearms aching from the impact, which gave him just enough time to whack my left knee and send me staggering backward.

"What the hell," I said again. "I gave you the computer."

"That's for the Illinois game, your senior year, shithead. I lost a hundred bucks on you."

"What are you talking about?" I said.

"Should have been an easy bet. Didn't know you were playing both sides."

The bat swung again, this time hitting my right forearm as I tried to shield my head.

"Fuck-up," he said. "That's all you are."

"Get a life," I managed. "That was twenty years ago."

"And that's how long I've been wanting to beat the shit out of you."

"It was a football game. Get over it."

"Woody Hayes, fuck-up," he said, swinging the bat once more.

Maybe it was the pain in my arms and knee. Maybe I was pissed at hearing the old nickname. Maybe it was the laptop. For whatever reason, I found myself summoning the best approximation of a quarterback feint I had left, grabbed the end of the bat as it bounced off the brick instead of one of my body parts, then gripped hard and pulled my unknown assailant toward me. Surprised, he stumbled forward and fell in front of me. I reached over and ripped off the ski mask. A stranger stared back. A tough-looking guy with a menacing goatee and shaved head and what looked like a missing front tooth. There was nothing remarkable about his face except for what was tattooed from his left ear all the way down his neck, a design you don't see every day, even in a football-crazy town like Columbus, Ohio.

He had put the shotgun and computer down to play out his revenge fantasy, so I had one shot to get this right. I raised the bat and took a step forward as I prepared to inflict a return blow, and that's all it took for my left knee, which has always been a bit tricky, especially when clobbered with my own Louisville slugger, to buckle. As I teetered backward he yanked the bat out of my hands and hit the knee again, sending me down hard. After that, the last things I remember were a string of his swear words interspersed with the word "fuck-up," then another voice that wasn't his or mine and might have been shouting something like "Hey—what are you doing?!"— and then something hard and sharp hitting my head, which just might have been one of his boots. I know it's a cliché, but it's also true: everything went black.

What's not a cliché is what happened next. I didn't wake up in a hospital or on somebody's couch or in the back of somebody's car trunk, bound and trussed. I woke up exactly where I'd fallen, probably not more than ten minutes later, to the taste of blood in my mouth, the sound someplace close of sirens, and my bat lying on the curb in front of me. I tried to get up, lay back down, then remembered the laptop, pushed myself onto my knees, opened my eyes and looked around in the alley. Nothing doing. It was gone. Shit.

# 2

"ONE MORE TIME," I SAID TO THE MAN SITTING across from me. "What in God's name possessed you to go into that girl's room?"

A day earlier. I was sitting at a window table at Cup o' Joe in German Village, the all-brick neighborhood south of downtown I call home. The Sunday *Columbus Dispatch* was spread before me, my large black coffee was cooling beside it, and next to that sat an uneaten pumpkin muffin.

"I don't know," he said for the third or fourth time. "I wasn't thinking."

"Tell me something I don't know."

I have a certain Sunday morning ritual, and like most people I don't like it interrupted. Sleep in a little, wake up and slurp some coffee, get dressed without rushing, put a leash on Hopalong and walk him around the block, then stroll over to the coffee shop for round two, including some pastries, while I sit and read the paper. If I have time, I'll browse in one of the thirty-two rooms in the Book Loft next door, then make my way home in time to leave for an 11:30 a.m. appointment I'm not in the habit of missing.

But not today. I'd scarcely begun the paper's extensive account of the Ohio State football team's convincing victory over Penn State the day before when my cell phone went off. I didn't recognize the number.

"Hello? Is this Woody Hayes?" A man's voice.

"This is Andy Hayes," I said. "May I help you?"

"*Andy* Hayes?"

"Andy Hayes," I said patiently. A lot of my calls go like this.

"You're sure?"

"Positive. Woody Hayes died in 1987. You can look it up."

"You know what I mean."

"I wouldn't dare to presume. Did you need something?"

A moment of silence. Then he said, "The thing is, I'm in a bit of trouble. Wondering if I could talk to you."

"Always happy to talk. Any particular topic?"

"It's kind of a long story."

"It usually is. I'm free tomorrow morning."

"I was hoping for sooner."

"Sooner?"

"Like today."

"Today."

"Like, maybe, this morning."

I glanced at the paper. I still had Travel, Arts and Life, and Business to get through, and I was already thinking a third muffin wouldn't be such a bad idea. And then of course there was 11:30 a.m.

"Mind if I ask what kind of trouble?"

"It might be better to tell you about it in person. If that's OK. Is your office close?"

"You do know it's Sunday morning, right? Is it really that urgent?"

"Yes," he said. "Burke Cunningham recommended you. Said it was OK to call."

Of course Burke would say that. So now I was stuck: either get mad at Burke for siccing what could well be a paying client on me, or get mad at the client just because it wasn't the world's most convenient time to call. Decisions, decisions.

I told him where I was.

"Any place less public?" he said.

"Plenty of places," I said. "But this is where I am at the moment."

"Your office?"

"That would be my living room. Which is a little cluttered right now."

"OK," he said finally.

I added, "I'll be the grumpy-looking guy wearing—"

He interrupted. "I know what you look like."

Of course he did. Everyone did. Some days it seemed like I was the only person left who didn't recognize the guy in my bathroom mirror.

# 3

LESS THAN HALF AN HOUR LATER THE COFFEE shop door opened and a man who didn't look like he was enjoying a relaxing Sunday morning in mid-November walked in. White, age indeterminate but someplace in his early forties. Tall, or taller than me, anyway, sandy hair receding, a few extra pounds but otherwise pretty good looking. Black peacoat, unbuttoned, khakis and blue button-down shirt.

"Ted Hamilton," he said, stopping at my table.

"Nice to meet you," I said, shaking the proffered hand. "Coffee?"

He shook his head. "Last thing I need right now."

"So how can I help you?"

"It's bad," Hamilton said, sitting down. "I don't know what I was thinking."

I waited. It was a familiar type of conversation.

"If you can't help me, then what? I could be well and truly screwed."

"I won't know if I can help until I hear your story."

8

"OK," he said, pausing as he looked around the coffee shop. He took a breath. "It's like this. I dropped my daughter off at a party Friday night—I needed the car and she was going to get a ride home later. We know the parents, and they were inviting people to stay and have a drink."

"Where?"

"In the kitchen."

"No—the house, I mean. What part of town."

"Upper Arlington. Big place. Near the golf course."

"That where you live?"

"No. Girls go to school together. Columbus Prep. We live in Clintonville."

"Gotcha. Go on. You had a beer."

"Right," he said. "OK, maybe a couple beers. And I hadn't eaten yet. Big mistake. I've got this blood sugar thing. Anyway, before I left I had to use the bathroom. Somebody was in the downstairs one, so I went upstairs. You know? And after I was finished and came out, I bump into my daughter's friend. The one whose house it is."

"This is still upstairs?"

"Right. In the hallway."

"What's the girl's name."

"Jennifer. Jennifer Rawlings."

"OK."

"And she's like, really glad to see me. You know. 'Hey, Mr. Hamilton. How's it going? Whoa, I like that shirt. How's stuff at work.' That kind of thing."

"OK," I repeated. My ex-wives used to complain, rightfully, that I was slow on the uptake. But even I could see where this was headed.

"So we start chatting, about school and movies and whatever, and then she mentions she's got something she's been meaning to show me. In her room."

I sighed. Couldn't help myself.

"So we go in there, and God, I don't know, the next thing I know we're, ah, kissing, and she's really, like, sort of all over me."

"All over you."

"That's right."

"And you're pushing her away? Fighting the whole time?"

He looked down. "Not exactly."

"Then what happened?"

"Thing is," he said. "I was a little drunk. And she was, you know, really hot, if you want the truth. And things with my wife and me, lately . . ."

"Keep going."

"So we're kissing, and I mean she seems really turned on, and then just when I'm starting to think, you know, how far is this going, she pulls away. Says she hears someone."

"Did she?"

"I don't know. I just know it all stopped real fast after that. After a few seconds she told me I better go. So I did. Left immediately. Right down the stairs and out."

"Anybody see you leave?"

"No idea. I was in a haze at that point."

"I take it that wasn't the end of things, or we wouldn't be sitting here."

He shook his head. "Yesterday I was checking my e-mail, and I saw this message from someone I didn't recognize. Subject line said, 'You and Jennifer.' My stomach dropped. Didn't know what to think. Guessed maybe it was from her father or something."

"I'm guessing it wasn't."

"I click on it and there's a real short message. 'One thousand dollars by midnight Monday or this goes up on YouTube.'"

"That's it?"

"That's it. I click on the attachment and it's a video. A video of us. In that room. It's, it's crystal clear."

"Any idea who the e-mail's from?"

He shook his head again. "The address was just letters and numbers. I figured it was her. But then I realized somebody had to shoot the footage, unless she did it herself somehow, remotely."

"Any idea how they got your e-mail?"

"Who knows. Internet? School directory? It's out there."

I said, "May I see?"

He nodded. "Figured you'd ask." He pulled out his phone, tapped on the screen a few times, then handed it to me. He looked away while I watched.

There was no sound, but he was right about the picture quality. It was good, the images clear and crisp, embarrassingly so, and there was no mistaking it was him. And he was right: it was bad.

I looked up at him.

"What in God's name possessed you to go into that girl's room?"

"I don't know," he said. "I'm screwed, aren't I?"

"You've got a big problem, that's for sure. So let's start with the basics: any idea how old that girl is?"

"She's eighteen. I'm sure of that."

"How do you know?"

"She just had a birthday—my daughter went to her party."

"You're sure? Because if she's underage, then I have to report it to police and this conversation's over."

"I swear. I wouldn't—I wouldn't cross that line."

"Big of you."

"I know I made a mistake. That's why I'm here. I just want to know if there's anything you can do to fix this."

"It depends."

"On what?"

"On what you want me to do."

"I want you to help me."

"First way I can help is play the middleman and handle the money."

"You mean I should pay them?"

"That's right."

"That's not what I had in mind."

"Probably smart. Second way I can help is tell them, on your behalf, to fuck off."

"Run the risk of them posting it? No way."

"Why not? What's the worst that could happen?"

"Everything. Marriage. Ruin me at work."

"What do you do?"

"Government relations. Work for grocery stores and liquor outlets. Lobbyist, basically."

"Ever had this kind of problem before?"

"Never," he said. "That's why this is so bad."

"First time for everything."

He grimaced. "Anything else you can do?"

"Option three is I have a friendly conversation with this girl. Persuade her it's not in her best interest, and whoever else is involved, to move forward."

"You could do that? Get them to call it off? Get the video?"

I shook my head. "Not in this day and age. A copy of that video is sitting on a server someplace and somebody's laptop and probably a flash drive, and that's just for starters. It's always going to be out there. You're going to have to live with that. Best I can do is keep them from posting it."

"Jesus Christ," Hamilton said. "What's the good of any of this, then?"

"Good question. I can make a strong argument on your behalf, and we'll cross our fingers. That's about all we've got right now."

"There's no way you could fix this permanently?"

"If by permanently you mean wind the tape back, return to a moment when it hadn't happened, then no. You're going to have to accept the possibility that someday the video will surface."

He went silent. I dipped my muffin in my coffee, took a bite. Looked out the coffee shop window and saw two women jog past. A man walking his dog the other direction turned to check them out. Another jogger, a man, passed the dog walker and checked *him* out. Sunday in German Village.

I heard Hamilton say, "When could you start?"

"You still want to hire me?"

"Sure," he said. Then he added: "What other choice do I have?"

"What we already talked about. Go home and tell your wife. Even if you decide we go after them, try to stare them down, it's better that she knows now. I mean, if your marriage is something you think worth's saving."

"I can only imagine her reaction."

"Don't, then."

"Don't tell her?"

"Don't imagine. Just do it and hope to be surprised."

He thought about this for several seconds. Then he said, "If you don't mind me asking, you know who Art Schlichter is, right?"

I sighed. I got this question a lot. "Former Ohio State and NFL quarterback who lost everything to his gambling addiction. Yes, I know who Schlichter is. What does that have to do with anything?"

"Nothing, I guess."

"But you asked."

"There are some similarities. You know."

"Here's the difference," I said. "We both went to prison, but I'm the one sitting in a coffee shop on my day off trying to save your ass."

# 4

HAMILTON CHOSE DOOR NUMBER 3, THOUGH without telling his wife yet, while I'd attempt to make the problem go away as much as it was possible in the digital age. It wasn't the option I'd have picked, but I was now up by a $500 deposit plus $100 a day in expenses. I lingered after Hamilton left, gulped a bit more coffee and took another bite of my muffin. I had one task to do before I got to work, and I wasn't looking forward to it. I dialed the number from memory.

"Hello?" I could tell right away I had awakened her.

"It's Andy," I said. "Sorry to call this early."

"Damn right it's early," she said, and I didn't respond, despite the fact it was nearing ten.

Instead I said, "Something's come up. A job. Guy called me while I was having coffee this morning."

"You can't make it." A statement, not a question.

"I could lie and say there's still a chance. Or I might be there, but just a little late. But, you're right, I can't make it. I don't know how it's going to unfold. So I'll tell the truth."

"And you know how I feel about the truth."

"Absolutely."

"And you also know how I feel about broken promises."

"I'm sorry."

"And how I feel about that expression."

I didn't say anything.

"On that note," she said, "Goodbye."

The hardest thing was not knowing whether she was disappointed I couldn't make it. I knew I was.

At least, I think I was.

BACK IN THE HOUSE I rent on Mohawk Street, I started by searching Facebook for Jennifer Rawlings. I found the same pretty-looking blonde from the video, her page locked to outsiders. I thought about sending her a Facebook message, but that could cut either way: it might provoke a return call, or it might scare her off.

Not sure what else to do, I called the number for the only Rawlings I could find listed in Upper Arlington.

"Hello?" A woman's voice. Too old to be Jennifer.

"This is Mr. Weatherbee?" I said. "From the high school? For Jennifer?"

"She's not here right now. Something I can help with?"

"Wouldn't you know, our website's gone down and I've been getting calls and e-mails about the assignment—lot of kids say they can't access it, and it's due tomorrow. I thought I'd just pass on the details by phone. Quicker that way. Do you know what time she'll be home?"

"She didn't say. Could I take a message?"

"Might be easier if I just talked to her myself. Or maybe I'll e-mail her and you can just tell her to check that. As long as you think she'll see it in time."

"Oh, I'm sure she will. And I'll text her just to be sure. She's at the library, supposed to be doing homework. What class did you say this was for?"

"English history."

"What did you say your name was again?"

"How about I leave you my number?"

It's a funny thing, but over the years I've found that nothing allays suspicion on calls like this more than offering a way to contact me.

"Ah, sure," she said. "Just a moment."

When she returned to the phone, I gave her my cell number. "Nice speaking with you, Mrs. Rawlings. You have a nice day."

"You, too."

ONE OF THE THINGS I like about Columbus is that, as big a city as it's gotten to be, it still takes only about twenty minutes to get anywhere. And so it was that in almost exactly that amount of time I was driving up Tremont to the library in Upper Arlington. It was a tony old suburb full of comfortable houses, wide boulevards, tall trees, fine golf courses, stellar schools, and a Fourth of July parade that people start reserving lawn space for days ahead of time. It was a bit much at times—the 'burb's nickname, "Uppity Arlington," was not always undeserved—but its charms were hard to argue with. Jack Nicklaus grew up there, and Dave Thomas, the guy who founded Wendy's, called it home for forty years. My namesake, the real Woody Hayes, moved there after landing the Ohio State job in 1950.

Which was one of the reasons, the cost of real estate aside, why I'd never considered living there myself. Just wouldn't have worked out.

I eased my blue Honda Odyssey into an open space in the library parking lot, got out of the car, and headed for the entrance. Then I reconsidered and took a stroll around the lot instead. I wasn't exactly sure what I was looking for, but I found it anyway underneath a tree at the end of a row of cars: a gleaming new red Mini Cooper with the license plate "JENI KAR."

I walked into the library, went over to the information desk, and explained my situation. A minute later I heard the announcement over the PA system. And a few minutes after that Jennifer Rawlings walked up to the desk, wearing a tight white sweater, jeans that fit her quite nicely, and a frown that could have stopped Sherman's army.

"I'm really sorry," I said. "I dinged your car as I was pulling in. Do you have a sec—" I said, and gestured toward the door.

"Oh geez," she said, with no improvement to the frown.

"Sorry," I murmured, and we walked out together, the librarian at the desk casting a sympathetic look in my direction.

We walked without talking until we reached her car, at which point she stopped and demanded, "Where is it?"

I took two steps toward her. I said, "You're Jennifer Rawlings?"

"Yeah, that's me," she said. "How'd you know my—"

"Here's the deal," I said. "I'm going to talk for five minutes and you're going to listen. Interrupt me and I'll key the Michigan fight song into the driver's side door of your pretty little vehicle here. Understood?"

"I—" she began.

"I'm here on behalf of Ted Hamilton. I know all about the party. I've seen the e-mail and the video. I know what you're up to and what you're asking."

"I, I don't know what you're talking about," she tried.

"No interruptions, remember?" I said, jingling my keys. "What you're doing is extortion, and it's illegal. You can go to prison for it. You and whoever shot that video. But even worse is the publicity. Got any college plans? You can kiss them good-bye if this hits the papers."

She stared toward the library, not meeting my eyes. But at least she was listening.

"I can see how you thought this might be pretty easy. A simple way to make some quick cash, not that you look exactly poverty stricken. I'll wager Mr. Hamilton wasn't even the first. But all that's in the past. The situation is now like this. Mr. Hamilton, who I represent, is declining to meet your demand. If you choose to post the video, he and I will be at the county prosecutor's office and the local FBI headquarters and the Upper Arlington Police Department and the sheriff's and the dogcatcher's and whoever else I can think of before you've had three hits on the site. Am I making myself at all clear?"

She didn't say anything. Just looked at her car.

"On the other hand, should you choose to rethink your request, we'll simply walk away—on one condition. I want the video camera, the laptop, and every memory stick and external drive and mouse used in this undertaking. If I'm in a good mood when I'm done wiping them clean, you'll get them back."

I looked at her to see if I was getting through. She met my glance, then looked away.

"Unfortunately," I said, looking at my watch, "I can't be as generous with my deadline as you were. Therefore, you have until eight o'clock tomorrow morning. If I don't have the stuff by then, I'll assume you're not accepting my offer and we'll head to the police. Got it?"

After a moment, she said, slowly, "I really don't know what you're talking about."

"That's up to you," I said. I reached into my wallet, pulled out my business card, and handed it to her. She wouldn't take it, so I tucked it under a windshield wiper on her car.

"Eight a.m.," I said. "Thanks for your time."

# 5

SINCE IT WAS BY NOW WELL PAST 2 P.M., I
drove back down the road, pulled into the Tremont Center lot,
and walked into the Chef-O-Nette. I sat at the counter and
declined the menu the waitress brought by.

"I'll have the Hangover," I said.

A few minutes later she brought me the restaurant's sig-
nature sandwich, consisting of a hamburger, slice of ham,
cheese, onion, lettuce, and tomato. I'd been there when I'd
needed the sandwich for the real thing. Today I just felt hungry. Fixing Hamilton's problem had given me an unexpected
appetite. But I got no further than my first bite when my
phone rang.

"Yeah," a boy's voice said. "This is, ah . . . Did you talk to
Jennifer Rawlings, like, a few minutes ago?"

"That's right."

"Did you, like, talk to her about Ted Hamilton."

"That's right," I said again.

"Did you ask her to give you something?"

"Right again."

"I think I've got what you want. If what you told her is true."

"I told her a lot of things."

"What you told her about the police."

"What I told her about the police is true."

"And you get the equipment, you won't tell the police."

"With a couple conditions."

"Conditions?"

"If the video ever surfaces, no matter how or who's responsible, the deal's off."

"All right, I guess."

"No," I corrected him. "All right, period. Secondly, the equipment has to check out. If you give me dummies or decoys, that's just going to increase your liability, because then you're looking at obstruction of justice."

"Can we get the stuff back?"

"Once I wipe everything, sure. No promises on how long that'll take."

"When can I give them to you?"

"Where do you live?"

"New Albany."

"That's clear across town. How do you know Jennifer?"

"We met at a tennis camp."

"Of course you did. What's your name."

He hesitated. "Do I have to tell you that?"

"Don't be stupid. And don't bother making it up. Your number is showing up on my phone. I can figure it out anyway in about two minutes."

"Pete," he said after a moment. "Pete Freeley."

"All right, Pete Freeley. Jennifer your girlfriend?"

A pause. "Yeah."

"A slutty extortionist. Cute."

"Listen—" he started.

"No, you listen. We'll do it at Easton. There's a surface parking lot near the Barnes and Noble. Nice and exposed."

"OK," he said. "What time."

"I'm right in the middle of something," I said. "Ninety minutes. Don't be late. And come alone."

"All right," he said.

I cut the connection and signaled the waitress.

"Tapioca pudding?" she said. "Best in town."

"Only if you can box it up," I said. "Sandwich too."

"Seems a shame to hurry on a Sunday afternoon."

"Truer words," I said.

# 6

TRAFFIC WAS LIGHT, EVEN FOR A SUNDAY, and I made it to Easton in, well, less than twenty minutes. "Mall" doesn't quite do the layout of Easton Town Center justice. The traditional indoor profusion of shops is bookended by two faux Main Street outdoor shopping areas. They're meant to evoke an old-fashioned downtown retail excursion but in fact bear about as much resemblance to a traditional city center as a golf course does to a wildlife preserve. All it did was remind me that as a boy, not all that long ago, the big deal in my little Ohio town was coming into Columbus to shop at the downtown Lazarus. And now Lazarus is gone too: not even Easton could bring it back to life.

I parked and got out of the van. I was exactly one hour early. Just the way I'd planned. I looked around and didn't see anyone meeting the description of a nervous teenager with a couple thousand dollars of electronic equipment in tow. I strolled over to a Panera, bought a cup of coffee and a *New York Times,* took both outside, found a bench with a clear view of the cars coming in and out of the lot, and waited.

I'd made it through the front section and sports—the *Times* was already weighing in on Ohio State's chances against Michigan in two weeks (good)—and I was deciding whether to go with Business or Arts when my mark showed up fifteen minutes early in a new-looking Explorer. We hadn't arranged a signal, but there was no mistaking the strained look on Freeley's face as he climbed out of the SUV.

As unobtrusively as possible, I got up from the bench and slipped back inside the restaurant. I found an empty chair at an inner wall table where I could see him but he couldn't return the favor. I watched as Freeley walked up and down the parking lot, trying to look as casual as possible. I waited another minute, found his number on my phone, and called him.

"Hello," he said sullenly.

"Listen very carefully," I said.

A minute later Freeley opened the back of his Explorer and pulled out a cardboard box. He walked over to the restaurant, set the box down on the bench where I'd been sitting a few minutes before, looked around uncertainly, then walked slowly back to his car and got in.

"Hello," he said, just as sullenly as before, when I called him back.

"Username and password?"

"Acooper. JarJarBinksMustDie."

"Who's Acooper?"

"I don't know."

"You don't know?"

"I borrowed the laptop from my dad. The name and password were taped to the bottom."

"Password is 'JarJarBinksMustDie'? Like in *Star Wars*?"

"I guess."

"You put this on a borrowed laptop?"

"It was just a joke," he said, weakly.

"Sure it was," I said. "OK—we're done here. Go home and stop thinking about it. I'll call you when I'm ready. Got it?"

"Yeah."

"Don't screw this up, Pete," I said. "Your future depends on it."

I waited for a count of twenty after he pulled out of the parking lot, then left the restaurant. I knew I didn't have a lot of time. You don't leave boxes on benches in public anymore without risking a visit from fire trucks and guys in hazmat suits. I picked the box up, walked to my van, set it down, opened the rear door, slid the box inside, shut the door, locked the car, and went back to sit on the bench. It was a nice day: cool but sunny, and it seemed a shame to be inside.

When fifteen minutes had passed I called Hamilton.

"Hello?"

"It's Andy Hayes."

"Oh right," he said distantly. "Can you hang on a second?"

So I hung on a second, which turned out to be almost a minute.

"Sorry," he said, returning to the line. "Couldn't talk just then." A whisper. "In the living room. With the wife." Then, louder: "What—what's up?"

I explained the situation. After a long pause, he said, "That was fast."

"It worked out."

After another pause he said, "I just wish we could be more sure. I mean, about the video."

"Me too," I said. "Sorry."

"So what's next?"

"Next is I check out the equipment, see how honest they were, then wipe everything. Couple of days, tops. After that, we hold our breath." *For the rest of your life,* I thought, but didn't say it.

"OK," he said.

"I'll call you by Tuesday. That'll be enough time."

"Tuesday," he said.

"Things change," I said, "we may have to renew the contract. But hopefully we're almost done."

"OK," he said again. He sounded distant now, and I thought I could hear a voice in the background.

"Bye now," I said, and hung up.

I waited another minute, then dialed the same number from memory I'd called earlier in the day.

"Hello?"

I said, "I know this is irregular, but any chance there's still room on your docket today? It turns out I'm just around the corner."

A long pause. I was getting a lot of those today.

"That is irregular," she said. "But not unprecedented. I suppose I could take your motion under advisement. How far away are you?"

"Ten minutes."

"How convenient. No way to be late."

I tried to think of something to say. But she had already hung up.

# 7

I DROVE OUT OF THE PARKING LOT, maneuvered onto Easton Way, then turned right on Stelzer Road. A couple of minutes later I pulled into a small subdivision of town homes. After parking the Odyssey in its usual spot, I walked to the door, knocked twice, paused, knocked again, then used my key to let myself in.

"Laura?" I said.

I'd learned the hard way she didn't like to be called "Judge," at least by me. I also knew she didn't want to be bothered with the niceties of answering the door. The key was her idea.

"In here," she said.

"Here," I knew, meant her study, which is where I found her at her computer.

"Sometimes," she said, without turning around at my entrance, "I am amazed how anyone made it through law school. I have never seen such weak, poorly constructed arguments in my life."

"Motion sickness?" I said, repeating her inside joke.

"Now they're asking to suppress another boxful of evidence. Like I haven't bent over backward already to what are sketchy requests at best."

"You're so exacting," I said as I leaned over and kissed her on the neck.

"Wait," she said, a little stiffly.

Had this been a few hours earlier, at our usual Sunday morning time, I would have persisted. But now, according to the parameters of our relationship, she had the upper hand because I'd screwed things up by canceling. I retreated to her bedroom, an austere room of beige walls and white curtains and gray carpet, sat down on the edge of the bed, picked up a copy of *Ohio Lawyer* on her nightstand, and read until, about five minutes later, she joined me. Then, for the next thirty minutes, with the door shut and the shades drawn, the judge's standoffish courtroom demeanor thawed into something close to affability. Afterward, I watched as she nonchalantly pulled her bathrobe back on without a word. She kissed me on the cheek, left the bedroom, and headed straight back to the study and likely the very same paragraph she'd been working on when I arrived.

I returned the kiss as I left.

"That was nice," I said.

"I should find you in contempt of court," she said.

"Your Honor's indulgence is appreciated."

As I got back into the Odyssey I remembered my partially eaten sandwich from Chef-O-Nette and realized how hungry I was. It was now approaching dinnertime, and my mood turned dark. If ours had been a normal relationship, I would have suggested to the judge—to Laura—that we get something to eat.

But ours was as far from a normal relationship as you could get in town. And so I glumly drove away.

BACK IN GERMAN VILLAGE, I stopped at Happy Dragon on Livingston for takeout Hunan beef. When I got home, despite my growling stomach, I emptied the dinner into a casserole dish and placed it in the oven on low heat. Then I dug a plastic bag out of a drawer, grabbed the leash, and took Hopalong, whose youthful golden lab friskiness had mellowed to amiable boredom in recent years, to Schiller Park. Not that I was counting, but I passed five different couples, three straight, two gay, enjoying each other's company in public. I did the math, figuring out the last time I'd had a real date. It wasn't pretty.

Back inside, I dumped my dinner onto a plate, cracked open a can of Black Label, and settled into my armchair. As I ate, I made some progress on Walter Isaacson's biography of Steve Jobs, which I'd picked up at the library a couple days earlier. An empty plate and three chapters later, I set the book down and channel-surfed for a while until I settled on ESPN and some of the pro game highlights. A brief segue into college games focused on the upcoming Ohio State–Wisconsin matchup. The Buckeyes were a three-point favorite.

After dinner I left the plate in the sink and took Pete's laptop out of the cardboard box. A Dell, newer model, with an Ohio State sticker on the upper left-hand corner. I powered it up, entered "Acooper" and the password "JarJarBinksMustDie," and started looking. I'm no computer guru, but it wasn't hard to find his handiwork, which he'd stored, rather charmingly, in a subfolder on the desktop named "JR" inside a subfolder named "Health Class" inside a folder named "Pete's Homework." I should have deleted the video then and there, but instead moved on to the video camera itself. I clicked through several options and took two accidental clips of my kitchen wall until I was satisfied the storage card was clear. The remaining question, whether he'd secretly stored the files elsewhere, on a flash drive or another computer or in the cloud, had to remain unanswered. I had no faith in taking him at his word, but lacking subpoena power, I had no way to do anything more about it.

It was a risky contest, since the one with the most to lose if Pete called my bluff about criminal charges was Ted Hamilton. And despite my best efforts, Hamilton was the lecherous equivalent of an uninsured driver. If Pete decided to, he could cause a very bad accident for him.

# 8

WHEN MY EYES OPENED AT 5:30 MONDAY
morning, I knew going back to sleep would be impossible.
Once upon a time I could crash until noon without rolling
over, but an untold number of on-field tackles and quite a few
off-field ones in subsequent years had put an end to that. My
joints acted as their own internal alarms.

After a single cup of coffee, black, and a look at the morning paper, I threw on my sweats, laced up my running shoes,
grabbed the leash, and headed back to Schiller Park with
Hopalong. After four laps around, or a little more than three
miles, I'd worked up a decent sweat. When I got back I checked
my cell phone and saw that I had three missed calls. I was starting to check voicemail when the phone rang again.

"This is Andy."

"It's Pete. Pete Freeley."

"It's not ready," I said. "I told you it would be a couple days."

"Didn't you get my messages?"

"I was jogging. You should give it a try. You seem like you
could use a little exercise."

"I need to talk."

I looked at my watch. "It's 8:00. Why are you calling so early?"

"There's been a mistake."

"Tell me about it."

"That's not what I mean. The laptop—there's something else on it. Something my dad needs. It's got nothing to do with what we talked about. With Jennifer, or anything like that. But it's really important."

"What is it?"

"I have no idea. Files of some kind. He says it's crucial he gets them back. He's going crazy."

"Can you be any more specific?"

"No—I don't know what they are."

"He didn't tell you?"

"No," he said, loudly. "He just said they were really, really important."

"Do you know where on the computer they are?"

"Listen, could I just come and take it? Just for an hour. I promise I'll bring it right back."

"You've got to be kidding."

"You have to help me, man. This is serious."

"Don't call me man. And it's serious to Ted Hamilton, too."

"It's not like that. I've never seen my dad like this."

"Listen carefully. I'm going to look at the computer, and I'm going to see what's on there. And then I'm going to wipe it. And then I'll call you back."

"Please," Pete Freeley said. "Don't wipe it yet. Please. What's the big deal? You've got the stuff. I'm just asking you to wait."

"No promises," I said. I waited, but there was no response. He'd hung up.

I LIFTED WEIGHTS FOR a couple of minutes in my living room while I thought about what to do. Then I showered, dressed, ate three bowls of cereal and a banana, rinsed and washed my bowl, then sat back down in front of the laptop.

I started by searching Word documents, with zero results, unless you counted what looked like a dozen or more English composition papers. Seemed like a lot for a high school kid, but I decided to stick to one mystery at a time. I moved on to PDFs: same outcome. But that wasn't saying much. I know my way around the basics of a computer, but nothing fancy. Freeley's father could easily have hidden files somewhere that would have been off-limits to me.

I finally thought I'd found something when I opened Excel and pulled up a spreadsheet crowded with number-filled cells. The headers had some categories I understood, like *provider, address, phone number;* some things I was a little vague on, like *receivables* and *credit reserve;* and some things that might as well have been Sanskrit, like *overcollateralization.* I looked a little farther and saw what appeared to be duplicates of the file, or maybe updates, but they meant nothing. It was all just numbers. Was this what Pete was talking about? Who knew?

Pete didn't answer when I called back. I found this odd until I realized it was a school day and he was probably in class. I left a message, then decided to text him as well: "Found bunch of files, can't tell one from another. Can't give u laptop yet. I'll be in touch."

I was pouring myself another cup of coffee and deciding my next move when my phone rang. I looked down, expecting Pete's number, but it was a caller I didn't recognize.

"Hello, yes. Andy *Hayes?*"

"That's right."

"Andy Hayes, *private* investigator?"

"Right again."

"This is, uh, someone, that is, someone interested in hiring you. If that's the right word."

The male caller had a hint of a southern accent and a formal lilt to his voice.

"That would be the right word. Unless 'engaging your services' is more your style."

"Do you, that is, would you undertake investigations of a sensitive matter?"

"Generally, there's no other kind."

"And you can be discreet?"

"It's called *private eye* for a reason," I said. "As long as you're not asking me to break the law."

"No, nothing like that," he said. "Is it possible we could meet?"

"Yes," I said. "But for that I'd need your name."

"That's necessary, I suppose."

"No name, no meeting."

"I understand. Well, in that case, this is Henry Huntington." A pause followed, almost as if he were hoping for a note of recognition from me.

"Nice to meet you, Mr. Huntington," I said.

"It's Dr. Huntington, actually," he said.

"Dr. Huntington, then. Where would you like to meet."

"Do you know the Top? The steak house? On East Main?"

"Of course."

"Perhaps we could have a cocktail together. This afternoon?"

"What time?"

"Say, five o'clock."

"Five o'clock," I said.

"Thank you," he said.

After I cut the connection I did what any other self-respecting private eye would do. I fired up my own laptop, opened a browser, and tried to figure out if I should know who Dr. Henry Huntington was.

# 9

NOT TWO MINUTES LATER THE PHONE RANG again. I wasn't used to such busy mornings.

"Mr. Hayes?" A man's voice.

"Yes."

"My name's Doug Freeley. I think you know my son Pete."

"That's right," I said. "Old buddies, Pete and me."

The slightest pause on his end. "I was wondering if I might have a word with you," he said. "In person."

"About what?"

"About the laptop."

"What about the laptop?"

"About getting it back."

"Not possible right now."

"The thing is, Pete needs it for school. And, well, there were some files of mine on there that Pete didn't quite know about. Some things for work I need back."

I said, "Pete needs the laptop for school?"

"That's right. I know what he did was wrong. But I don't think that gave you the right to take it. Be that as it may, we're not interested in making a big fuss or anything. I'd just like it back."

"What did Pete tell you he did?"

"What did he tell me?"

"You heard me."

"I'm not sure it's necessary to repeat all that."

"I think it is."

"Well, if you insist"—an aggrieved tone crept into his voice—"he said he was at the mall, at Easton, with some friends, and they were using the mall wireless to, well, to download pornography. Stream it. And then you saw them and told them they'd broken mall rules and you'd have to confiscate it."

"I saw them?"

"That's what he said."

"Who did he tell you I was?"

"Some kind of undercover mall security officer."

"He told you I was a security guard?"

Another pause. "Well, aren't you?"

I sighed. "Where do you live?"

He told me.

"I'll be there as soon as I can."

"With the laptop?"

"I'll see you soon," I said, and hung up.

I WAS MOVING UP in the world of suburbs: the Free-leys lived in New Albany on the far east side. It was a village once, but the residents now included billionaires, like the guy who founded the Limited. I retrieved my van, caught the NPR headlines update on WCBE, the local independent radio station, then settled in for the station's morning world music program. It was the perfect accompaniment for my expedition east. After several minutes on a series of highways, I exited onto Dublin-Granville Road, turned down Greensward Road, and soon found myself passing large red-brick houses with double wings and U-shaped driveways and multicar garages in the back. I pulled in behind a pair of Escalades parked in front of the Freeleys' house, one white, one black.

I hadn't even made it up the walk when the door opened and an older, slightly taller version of Pete Freeley stepped out. Doug Freeley was distinguished looking, with short dark hair starting to gray, blue eyes, and a chiseled, handsome face. Pin-striped suit, white shirt, dark-patterned tie. He looked to the right and left, making sure we weren't noticed, before making eye contact and reaching out his hand. If he recognized me, he didn't show it.

"Thanks for coming," he said.

Inside, he guided me into a living room nearly the size of my house. He gestured to a large black leather L-shaped sectional couch, where I sat down, flipping an Ohio State throw pillow aside, and admired the fireplace opposite me. Mrs. Freeley—"Beth," Doug Freeley said with a vague wave in her direction—delivered a tray of steaming coffee cups, cream and sugar, then stood on the periphery. There was no sign of Pete.

"No trouble finding us?" Doug Freeley said.

"None," I said. "So he told you I was a mall cop?"

He shifted in his seat and looked uncomfortably at his wife, then back at me. He was sitting on the far side of the sectional, as far away from me as it was possible to sit without falling off the couch. Or being pushed. He gripped his cup of coffee as though someone might take it from him.

"That's right."

"And he was stealing wireless to download porn?"

"That's what he said."

"You realize he could do that at home? And being a teenage boy, probably already has? And probably on a smart phone, which arguably has better screen resolution than that laptop."

"I just—I'm just telling you what he said."

"Did he say anything else?"

"Not really. He apologized. Said he was sorry."

"Where is he?"

Beth spoke. "Still at school," she said. She was pretty, dyed blonde but tasteful, smart in gray leggings and a brown knit dress accented with a wide leather belt and boots to match, with a trim figure to equal her husband's. They were a striking couple.

"Did he know I was coming?"

"No," she said.

"How'd you get my number?"

"He gave it to us," Doug said. "After I started asking about the laptop."

"What's on the computer that's so important?"

"Work files," he said. "Things from the office I needed at home."

"Not on a flash drive? Seems more convenient than lugging around a laptop."

"Easier this way," he said, a little vaguely. "I was afraid I might lose a flash drive."

"As opposed to losing a laptop," I said.

"Well, right," he said.

"Where do you work?"

Freeley shifted again, and again traded glances with his wife. I might have been mistaken, but the look did not seem to be what we in the trade call lovey-dovey. "American Financial Health Care."

"Never heard of it."

"Most people haven't."

"What do you do?"

"It's a bit complicated."

"Try me."

"We help small health care facilities, like nursing homes or doctors' practices, pay their bills faster. Something like that."

"Sounds simple enough. What kind of files were on the laptop?"

"Important ones," he said.

"How important?"

"The thing is," Freeley said, ignoring my question, "Pete got ahold of the laptop without me knowing and went off to the mall. Which is where you came in."

"No," I said. "It's not."

"I'm sorry?"

"That's not where I came in."

"What do you mean?"

I took a sip of the coffee Beth had placed before me.

I said, "Let me explain a couple of things."

THERE WAS A LONG silence when I'd finished.

"I don't believe it," Doug said, in a tone that suggested the opposite. He looked at Beth, who had sat down in a wingback chair near the fireplace. She just shook her head.

"What can I do to fix this?" Doug said. "I really need the laptop back."

"You'll get it back. But it's not going to be right away. I need to deal with the video files, see what else Pete might have stored on there that might relate to my client. You'll forgive me if I don't take his word that he told me everything."

"I can pay," Doug said. "If that's what it takes. How much? A thousand? Two thousand? I'll write you a check right now."

"It's not about money," I said.

"I really need those files."

"I agree with Doug," Beth interrupted, impatience in her voice. "Those files mean a lot to his company. Seems like you could do what you have to do with the video in an hour or two."

"Might seem like it," I said. "But it's just going to take a little longer."

"We could call the police," Beth said, color rising in her cheeks.

"You could," I agreed. "And I could be sure to mention up-front the reason I have the laptop at all."

"That won't be necessary," Doug said quickly.

Beth started to speak, then stopped. She appeared to be wrestling with something. Whatever it was stayed unspoken, though if I'd had to guess, it didn't involve a charitable thought toward her husband. "You're right," she said after a moment. "Against my better judgment, I'll trust Mr. Hayes on this." She wouldn't meet my eyes as she said my name. "Right now, we've got other things to worry about. We've got to deal with Pete. This is . . . unacceptable. Completely unacceptable behavior."

"Unacceptable," Doug echoed a moment later..

"Just give me a few days," I said. "I'll call you as soon as I can."

"Please," Doug said. "As quickly as possible."

"A few days will be fine," Beth said. "We appreciate everything you've done. I'm sorry about our son."

"Not as sorry as my client," I said.

# 10

I WAS STILL TRYING TO WRAP MY MIND
around the parenting issues confronting the Freeleys when I
walked under the long white awning at the Top that afternoon
and looked around.

I wasn't sure quite what I'd expected Henry Huntington
to look like. After collecting information from my Google
search, I'd tried to put aside whatever stereotypes I had about
the result: provost and distinguished professor of nineteenth-
century American studies at McCulloh College, a small liberal
arts institution tucked between the city's other two east-side
colleges, Capital and Ohio Dominican. On the one hand, the
man who stood up as soon as I'd reached the bar was indeed
wearing a bow tie, tortoiseshell horn-rimmed glasses, and a
tweedy-looking jacket with the requisite elbow patches. On
the other hand, his hair was longer than I would have guessed,
nearly shoulder length, and the close attention he was paying
his smart phone as I walked up—and indeed paid throughout
our conversation—belied any notions of a fusty academic out
of step with the modern age. Frankly, he looked right at home

with the smart set crowding the bar at the Top, an old-style steak house on East Main Street.

"Mr. Hayes," he said, extending a hand.

"Call me Andy," I said.

The bartender approached and I ordered an Elevator Brewing Company Buckeye Red draft. Huntington signaled for a second bourbon on ice. Cocktail hour was in full swing, and the bar was getting loud. I signaled toward a table and he nodded. We walked past the piano player and tucked into a corner booth.

"A shame there's so few of these places left," he said. "It's like a tableau of the elegant past."

"I try not to dwell in the past," I said.

"An optimist?"

"Something like that. What can I do for you?"

"Regrettably," Huntington said, looking past me, "I believe my wife is having an affair. I'd like you to look into it."

"What makes you think that?"

"Inklings," he said. "She doesn't work, well, not for money, and there are stretches of the day where I can never seem to reach her. Especially between noon and two. Monday, Wednesday, Friday. Like clockwork." He sipped his drink. I followed suit.

"Don't get me wrong," he said, responding to something in my expression. "She occupies herself fully. She sits on the boards of the art museum and the conservatory, and she hosts a number of faculty gatherings at our house each semester. As you can imagine, those can rival Yalta in their social complexity."

I nodded, unable to imagine this.

"Hester and Roger also require a fair amount of work on her part."

"Your children?"

"Our poodles."

"Toy?"

"Standard," he said, sounding slightly offended.

"You're a Hawthorne scholar?"

"You know my work," he said.

"I know my *Scarlet Letter* characters."

"Very good," Huntington said.

"Not as good as a husband and wife in your circumstances having poodles with those names. But you were saying."

"Yes," he said, a tad frostily. "In any case, she does have time on her hands. As I said, between noon and two three days a week, it's a blank canvas. Her answers are vague, evasive, if I press her on where she was."

"What's her name?"

"Honey."

"That's her Christian name?"

"Her given name is Susan. But no one knows her by that."

"Have you asked her?"

"Asked her?"

"If she's having an affair."

"Not in so many words. But I suspect she knows I suspect something."

"What would you like me to do?"

"Discover the truth," he said. "See where she goes, what she's doing. What his name is, if my suspicions are right."

"And then?"

"Bring the information to me, of course."

"What will you do with it?"

"I suppose I haven't completely decided yet. Frankly, I'm hoping you'll prove me wrong."

I explained my fee structure. If he found fault with the amounts, his expression didn't show it.

"One other thing," I said.

"Yes?"

"I don't take sides in these cases. I just provide information. What you do with it is your business. As long as it doesn't involve violent behavior toward your spouse. Am I making myself clear?"

"Perfectly," he said.

I walked out of the Top $500 richer than when I'd walked in, but still not sure how I felt about the job. There was something about Huntington that bugged me. Despite his good looks, station in life, and apparent access to lots of cash, I could see why his wife might not be entirely happy at home.

# 11

I WAS SHORT ON GROCERIES—YESTERDAY'S
activities had interrupted my usual supply run—so I stopped
by the Giant Eagle off Whittier, the one that used to be the Big
Bear, before returning to my house. By then Hopalong was
whining for his walk. I took him around the park once, then
headed home, hungry.

The first thing I noticed as I neared home was the police
cruiser parked in front of the house, followed by the police
officer standing on my porch writing something in a notebook. Beside him was my twenty-something neighbor in a
jogging suit.

"Everything OK?" I said.

The officer looked at me for a moment longer than necessary, then glanced at something in his notebook.

"You live here?"

"Yes."

"You got broken into."

"You're kidding."

"Went through the back door. This girl here heard something, called it in. You mind taking a look inside, see if anything was taken."

I looked at my neighbor. I said, "You all right?"

She nodded. "I was just coming back from running. I wouldn't normally go around the back, but I'd picked up some trash by the park and came around to the alley to throw it in the garbage. I noticed when I walked past your house that the back door was partly open. I didn't think anything of it at first. But after I dumped the stuff, I was walking back and these two guys came out of the door, moving kind of fast. They looked at me and just took off." She pointed vaguely up the street. "I got a little closer and saw the door had been forced open. That's when I called the police."

"Thanks," I said.

The officer gestured toward my front door. "You mind?"

Inside, I moved slowly from room to room, turning on lights as I went. No question somebody had been there. Stuff was thrown everywhere. Pillows were off the couch, magazines from my coffee table littered the floor, and my desk was a mess. Thanks to the generosity of a former client, I was able to rent a house in German Village at below the normal sky-high rate, but the heady real estate prices didn't insulate the neighborhood from the usual rash of property crime. It was still the city, after all. Yet the longer I looked, the more it became clear they were either the world's worst burglars or they were after something else. My TV was still there. So was my own laptop, though it would have taken an enterprising pair of B&E men to find where I keep it hidden under my bed—the unfortunate consequence of a series of neighborhood break-ins the year before. I wondered if it would have mattered. The loose change on the top of my dresser was right where I'd left it. I walked through twice but my conclusion didn't change. Someone had broken in, ransacked the place, then left without taking anything discernible.

"You sure?" the cop asked.

"I'm sure," I said. "I don't have that much to begin with, and all the obvious stuff is here."

"Any prescription drugs?" he said. "Half the time these guys will skip the family silver and go straight to the medicine cabinet looking for Vicodin."

I shook my head. "Ibuprofen. Aspirin. Maybe some cough syrup."

"Kind of strange," he said.

"Maybe Shelley interrupted them?" I said, referring to my neighbor.

He thought about it. "Possible, I guess. But the way she made it sound, they looked like they were finished with the job when she saw them."

That's when I remembered. Just before leaving for the Freeleys' house I had stuck the laptop and the camera equipment in the back of the van in case they could serve some purpose in our meeting. They hadn't. But it was all still there. Not in the house.

"I dunno," I said slowly. "Maybe they were after drugs, then decided to hightail it when they came up empty."

"Doesn't explain why they left your TV."

"True," I said.

"You're Woody Hayes, aren't you?" the officer said. "If you don't mind me asking. I mean, I recognized you."

"I'm flattered," I said, which he and I both knew was a lie. "I go by Andy now. And no, I don't mind you asking."

"Andy," the officer said, considering. "Got anything from your playing days inside? Anything valuable?"

I shook my head. "All long gone."

"Still got your ring."

I saw he was looking at my hand. I raised the offending item: a Big Ten championship ring from a couple of decades ago.

"That's it," I said. "Not even sure why I still wear it."

"Worth a lot of money. Probably safer there."

"Maybe."

"People know you live here?"

"Some people," I said. "Why?"

"Just wondering if maybe you were targeted for, you know, who you were."

"Buckeye fans going a bit too far?" I said.

"Who knows. Heard of weirder things."

"Me too," I said.

"Michigan game in a couple weeks. People get strange ideas."

"Strange," I said. But he wasn't half wrong. The insults and heckling always go up the second half of November, right before the big game.

We left it at that because there wasn't anything else to do. I was the victim of a victimless crime, unless you counted the busted doorjamb and the mess inside. The officer took my essentials and gave me a case number. When he'd gone, I walked next door and knocked on Shelley's door and thanked her for calling the police.

"Did you lose much?" she said.

"Peace of mind."

I went inside and cleaned up as best I could. Took me an hour just to get the basics back in place.

It was past nine o'clock when I realized I still hadn't brought Pete's equipment inside. Making sure the broken door would at least stay closed, if not locked, I headed out to retrieve it.

Like a lot of people, I love German Village and hate the parking hassles that can come with it. On rare occasions the stars align and I'll find a space along Mohawk near my house. But more often than not, I end up following a tiresome routine: drive down to Whittier, turn right, turn right on Lazelle and then right again on Lansing where I begin eyeballing empty spots. It could be worse, I suppose. For a guy whose college football past had brainwashed me to suspect all things

Michigan, Lansing wasn't quite as bad a name for the half-alley half-street as, say, Ann Arbor. And it was generally well lit, except for tonight, when one of the lights was out. But it felt, well, just a little lonelier on Lansing compared to Mohawk. It was, as I said, still the city.

After I got to the van, I opened up the rear, lifted out the box, put it on the ground, then reached farther in and retrieved my trusty baseball bat. I shut the door and hit the van's remote lock. Bat in hand, I picked up the box and had started walking up Lansing to Mohawk when I heard the sound behind me. Then came the voice.

"Hey! Woody Hayes!"

# 12

"YOUR LUCKY NIGHT," THE MAN STANDING over me was saying. "A burglary and an assault."

I said, "Maybe we should wrap this up so I can go buy a lottery ticket."

I was sitting on the side of an emergency room hospital bed in Grant Medical Center downtown. My head felt like someone had massaged it with the claw end of a hammer, my arms ached if I let them relax by my sides and ached even more if I lifted them off the bed, and my left knee did not appear to be working. On my left a nurse was swabbing something cold and stingy on my shoulder. "This is going to hurt," she said. "A lot."

"Honesty appreciated," I said.

"Shit," I said a second later. "You weren't lying."

"I haven't really started yet," she said.

In front of me stood Columbus police Detective Henry Fielding. Light reflected off his shiny white bald head, and I was pretty sure his nose, whenever it had been broken, had involved somebody's fist and not an accidental encounter with an errant door.

"You're a private investigator now." A statement.

"That's right."

"Ever seen that movie *Point Break?* Keanu Reeves is an ex–Ohio State quarterback who becomes an FBI agent."

"'Quarterback punk,'" I said. "Yes, I've seen *Point Break.* Except I'm not an FBI agent and this isn't Southern California. Next question."

"OK. Got a license?"

I fished it, very painfully, out of my wallet.

"Who do you work for?" Fielding asked.

"Burke Cunningham, mostly."

"Burke Cunningham? Guy who defends all the killers?"

"Alleged killers," I said.

"Figured you'd say that. Anybody else?"

"I freelance. People hire me on the side."

"Cunningham knows about those jobs?"

"Sure. Recommends people sometimes."

"Why do you freelance? Cunningham doesn't pay enough?"

"I have more than one ex-wife and two sons I pay a considerable sum in child support for. Happily pay, I might add. Mind explaining what all this has to do with anything?"

"Talked to the officer who took the report earlier," Fielding said, ignoring me. "Nothing missing from your house?"

"That's right."

"But this time they took a laptop?"

"That's right," I said again.

"But not your wallet."

"Apparently not."

"Any idea why they didn't take the computer the first time?"

"It was in my van," I said. "Forgot I'd left it there. I was retrieving it after the break-in."

"Lucky for you."

"Lucky?"

"Lucky it was in the van. At least the first time they came by."

"That's assuming it was the same people."

"Why wouldn't it be?"

"I don't know. There was only one guy in the alley. Gal next door saw two leave my house."

"Only one guy that you saw."

"I put up a little bit of a fight," I said. "I'm thinking a second guy would have jumped in to help."

"Waiting in a getaway car?" Fielding suggested.

"He wasn't dressed the same way."

"The same way?"

"This guy was in all dark clothes. The other guys were wearing gray sweatshirts."

"OK, same gang, third guy. You said it sounded like he knew who you were."

"Everybody knows who I am. The first nurse in here gave me a look like I kill puppies in my spare time."

"Do you?" said the nurse working on my shoulder.

"Only if their eyes aren't open yet," I said. "I'm sure he recognized me. You did, didn't you?"

"Anything important on the laptop," Fielding said, ignoring me again.

"Important enough," I said carefully. "Files, documents. The usual."

Fielding said, "I'm just wondering. A break-in, nothing taken. Pretty rare, in my book. An hour later, you're jumped and he leaves your wallet but grabs the one valuable thing that wasn't in the house earlier. Leaves a pretty nice video camera, too."

"OK."

"Just seems odd, is all." He waited. I didn't say anything. Problem was, I agreed with him.

I was starting to wonder whether it was time to come clean about Pete Freeley and Jennifer Rawlings when the nurse who'd been torturing my shoulder interrupted.

"Gotta take your pulse," she said.

"It's sixty-eight," I said.

"I beg your pardon?"

"I've got a resting pulse of sixty-eight."

"Thank you, Dr. Kildare," she said as she placed a small plastic clamp on the pointer finger on my left hand. That's when I noticed.

"My ring," I said.

Fielding said, "What?"

I raised my hand. The nurse told me in no uncertain terms not to.

"My ring. Big Ten champions."

"I remember," Fielding said.

"Me too," I said. "It's missing."

"When's the last time you saw it?"

"When the other officer asked me about it two hours ago. After the break-in."

"He didn't have it when he came in," the nurse concurred. "And your pulse is 69."

"Must be nervous," I said.

Fielding wrote some things in his notebook. He said: "Laptop, Big Ten ring."

"I got mugged," I offered.

"Or someone made it look like a mugging."

"Are you always like this?" I said.

"Like what."

"So conspiratorial."

"Only with gridiron heroes," he said, but without the slightest trace of humor in his voice.

"In that case, you've got the wrong guy."

GRANT IS NOT MUCH more than a mile from my house, and I thought briefly about walking after Fielding was done and I'd politely told Nurse Ratched I wouldn't be accepting the hospital's invitation to spend the night for observation, whatever that means. The pounding in my head dissuaded me from attempting the journey, along with the stab of pain in my side and the fact that my knee couldn't bend. I thought about calling a cab, but I was tired of strangers for the night. I considered asking Burke, but it didn't seem worth getting him out of bed, and I wasn't sure I wanted to explain about the laptop.

In the end I called Roy. He showed up about twenty minutes later in his battered white van with "Church of the Holy Apostolic Fire" emblazoned across the side. He had a backseat passenger, as was often the case. A woman looking as if she'd seen not just better days but better decades.

"Jesus," he said, looking at me. "You look worse than people I saw in Fallujah."

"Says the guy who left part of a leg there," I said, climbing slowly into the passenger seat.

"Had a spare," he said. "No big deal. Theresa," he said, gesturing behind him, "Andy. Andy—Theresa. I was just taking her home after church when you called."

"Mister, you got a cigarette?" Theresa said.

"I don't smoke."

"Pills?"

"Proselytizing going well?" I said to Roy.

"Baby steps," he replied, slowing for the light at Grant and Livingston. "Wasn't for me, she'd have spent her evening much differently."

I tried to think of something snappy to say but came up with fog. Just as well. Roy and his white van and storefront church were a do-gooding force of nature. Much more effective than a private investigator who couldn't hang onto one stinking laptop.

"So what happened?"

I explained, leaving out the same things I didn't tell the first officer or Fielding. Roy wasn't fooled.

"I'm thinking that's 50 percent of what really happened. "About right?"

"About," I said.

He pulled up in front of my house. "Need help getting in?" he said.

"No thanks. Look, I really appreciate the lift."

"You're welcome. Glad you called. I'll check in tomorrow."

I opened the door with difficulty. It was hard to say at this point if there was anything on me that wasn't hurting.

"Hey, mister," Theresa said.

"Yeah?"

"Let me come with you. Fifty bucks. All night."

I turned back to look at her. I said, "Listen to me. This guy here, Pastor Roy? Listen to what he says. Take his advice."

"Why should I?"

"Because he's the one guy in the whole city who's got your back but doesn't want you on it. You understand what I'm saying?"

She looked at me, blankly.

"You do that for me, listen to Roy and let him help you, and you and I will go get breakfast, on me, wherever you want. Just breakfast, though. And no cigarettes."

She continued looking at me as if I were a private investigator from another planet.

Roy interrupted. "Theresa's a little shy. And I've told her she has to stop trusting strange men."

"God knows why she's with you," I said, shutting the door with a wave.

Inside, I let Hopalong out to water my dead pansies, let him back in, then pushed a chair up against the knob of the back door and fastened the chain. Best I could do for tonight. I opened the fridge, pulled out my last Columbus Brewing Company Winter Warmer, and used it to wash down some of the Tylenol with codeine I'd left the emergency room with.

From there I somehow made it to my bedroom and found myself lying on my back. I managed to keep my eyes open for almost ten seconds before, for the second time that night, things just went black.

# 13

EVEN MY INTERNAL ALARM CLOCK COULDN'T
compete with a baseball-bat massage. I woke up at seven with
a raging headache and several aching body parts. It's possible
I'd taken worse overall beatings in my playing days, except they
hadn't involved muggings and I'd been twenty years younger. I
staggered to the bathroom, then lumbered around the kitchen
slowly, making coffee and feeding the dog. I let him back out
into my postage-stamp yard. A walk was out of the question.
Plus I had work to do.

"WHAT THE HELL?" Ted Hamilton said when I reached
him. "I hired you to get the laptop, not lose it."

"I didn't lose it," I said for the second time. "Somebody
took it."

"So what are you going to do about it?"

"I'm going to figure out who's got it and get it back. But
I'm not holding out a lot of hope right now. So many pawn-
shops, so little time, if you catch my drift."

"Very funny."

"Speaking of funny, OK if I rule you out as a suspect?"

"What are you talking about?"

"Just running down all the leads. You had a motive to make sure the laptop was secured."

"You think I was behind this?"

"I don't think anything. I'm just asking questions."

"You have a hell of a lot of nerve, you know that?"

"Maybe I do. And maybe that's why I was able to help you in the first place."

"Big help."

"Let me try it this way," I said. "Where were you last night?"

"Listen," he said, ignoring me. "If this video surfaces, I'm blaming you. I hired you to do something about it, and that didn't include losing the laptop as soon as you got it. You don't get it back, I'm going to make your life very difficult. Understand what I'm saying?"

"One more time," I said. "Where were you last night?"

"Go to hell," Hamilton said, and cut the connection.

Hamilton was angry, and probably rightfully so, I thought afterward, nursing my third cup of coffee. But you didn't need to be a private eye to figure out he hadn't answered my question.

A few minutes later I had a similar conversation with Doug Freeley. He didn't swear as much as Hamilton, but he was no less angry.

"All I'm saying," I tried to explain, "is the same day I meet you, and you explain how important that laptop is, somebody breaks into my house, and then a couple of hours later I'm jumped and the laptop's gone. I'm not saying you had anything to do with it. But I've got to check everything."

"If you say so," he said, before hanging up.

He didn't tell me where he was the night before either.

# 14

PEEVED, I WALKED FROM THE KITCHEN TO my living room and back a few times to let off steam. Calming down, I studied the splintered jamb on the back door, an unwelcome reminder of the night before, and an even more unwelcome reminder of my unfinished business: how to retrieve the Freeleys' laptop from an unknown assailant in a city where those kinds of robberies happened all too often and the merchandise was recovered in fewer than 1 percent of cases.

A knock at the door interrupted my attempt at exercising the power of positive thinking. *Now what,* I thought. Standing before me when I swung the door open was a woman a few years younger than me in a long, dark, padded winter coat, looking all business.

"Andy Hayes?"

"It depends," I said. "Are you here to beat me up too?"

"I don't know," she said. "Do you need beating up?" Her eyes went to the swollen left side of my face. "Oh dear," she said. "Moot question, I see. Are you all right?"

"I'll live. What can I do for you?"

She reached into the pocket of her coat, pulled out a business card and handed it to me.

"Special Agent Cindy Morris. Columbus FBI. Nice-looking dog."

I looked down. Hopalong had nosed his way beside me and was gazing with interest at a squirrel across the street.

I said, "The last government I tried overthrowing was a bunch of clowns on middle school student council. Promise."

"We know," she said, her face straight. Then, reading mine, she added, "Kidding."

"So I owe the pleasure to?"

"Possible for me to come in?"

Inviting an FBI agent into my home was about the last thing I wanted to do, especially after last night. But sometimes you just have to go with the flow.

"Nice house," she said when we entered the kitchen.

I ignored compliment number 2. "Don't take this the wrong way," I said, "but could you please state your business?" Without asking, I started making coffee. Maybe the caffeine would help my headache.

"Doug Freeley," she said. "You've been talking to him. Why?"

I measured two scoops of whole beans into the grinder and hit the start button. I let it go for twenty seconds or so, then raised my thumb off the button.

I said, "I think this is where I'm supposed to say, 'Who told you that?' or, 'Suppose I have been?'" I filled the Mr. Coffee carafe with six cups of water and carefully poured it into the coffee maker. "But I'll skip that part and go straight to 'So?'"

"So that's of interest to us."

"That's nice," I said. I turned the coffee on. I waited.

"We were just wondering what you might be talking to him about."

"That's annoying when you do that," I said.

"Do what?"

"Talk like the queen. 'That's of interest to *us*. *We* were just wondering.' You have an opinion of your own on this, Special Agent Morris?"

She studied my face. I studied hers. She had thick black hair pulled back with a plain black scrunchie, simple gold stud earrings, and the faintest traces of makeup. No glasses, but I was betting contacts. She was athletic looking, and if I had to guess, I'd say she played something like soccer or lacrosse when she was younger.

"Fair enough," she said. "I'm interested in knowing why you're talking to Doug Freeley."

"That's more like it," I said. "It's none of your business."

She smiled.

I said, "Anything else we can help you with today?"

She smiled again. "No interest in making this easy, Andy?"

"Since I don't have any idea what we're really talking about here, no, I guess not. Care to elaborate?"

"Probably not."

"Well, then."

"But we, that is to say, I am willing to make a small exception in your case."

"Nice of you." I opened the cupboard and examined my collection of coffee mugs. After deliberating a moment, I chose a commemorative DEA mug for myself and a similar ATF mug for my guest.

"Take anything in it?" I said.

"Black is fine," she said.

She continued, "This isn't rocket science, Andy. I'm guessing you know where Doug Freeley works. You can probably figure out why we might have an interest in him. And conversely, why we're interested in why a private detective is talking to him."

"Freeley works for American Financial Health Care. He does something with health care companies and bills. He lives in a darn nice house in New Albany, just like a zillion other white-collar success stories. What am I missing?"

"Other than why you were at his house the other day, I'm not sure."

I took a slug of coffee, burning my tongue in the process. But my head felt better almost as soon as the coffee went down my throat. "Back to my original answer," I said. "But since you've been nice enough to pay me a house call, I'll throw in a bonus response: it has nothing to do with American Financial."

She sipped her own coffee. "I find that hard to believe."

"Believe what you want," I said. "It's the truth."

"So it's pure coincidence that our, ah, *my* interest in Doug Freeley dovetails at almost the exact same time with your interest in him?"

"First of all, I'm guessing that your interest predates mine. Secondly, I have zero interest in Doug Freeley. I did talk to him recently, as your predator drones detected, and while I can't promise it was our last conversation, it may have been our second-to-last. He's tangentially connected to a case I'm working on, and he's certainly not the object of my investigation. For extra credit, I'll add that his son is involved in the case. And that's way, way more than I have any obligation to tell you."

"Tangentially," she said.

"Triple word score," I said. "You can look it up."

"What happened to you, anyway?" she said, gesturing at my face.

"I had a disagreement with someone."

She lifted an eyebrow.

"I got mugged last night."

"Are you all right?"

"I'll live to investigate another day."

She took another sip of coffee. "I was hoping we could work together. Maybe cooperate."

"Really," I said. "Tell me more."

"I was hoping you could tell me your interest in Doug, and that might help what we're doing. And I do mean, we."

"Sounds like a one-way street. What do I get out of this cooperation?"

"The satisfaction of helping your government?"

I laughed out loud.

"How about, a subpoena-free week?" But she was smiling, sort of, as she said it.

"If that's the way you want to play it, be my guest."

"It's not. But my options are dwindling."

"I'm not sure I agree."

"No?"

"I've only seen one option so far: make me tell you everything about what I'm doing, while telling me squat about what you're up to. So here's my counteroffer: come clean about your investigation into Doug Freeley and American Financial Health Care, including when you expect the first indictments, and I'll reconsider my position."

"Of course you know I can't do that."

"Give me a break. You're the FBI. You can do anything."

It was her turn to laugh.

I said, "Since neither of us is willing to punch the other's dance card, do you mind if we call it a day? I'm a little achy from last night and I have a lot to do. None of it involving Freeley, by the way."

"Nothing I can do to make you reconsider?"

"Other than make me a better offer?"

She put down the ATF mug. "Thanks for the coffee," she said.

"You're welcome," I said.

I walked her to the door. As I opened it, I said, "Soccer or lacrosse?"

"I beg your pardon?"

"You move like an athlete. You played a sport at some point."

"How private investigator-ly of you," she said. "Field hockey, in fact." She added: "I wielded a mighty stick."

I was about to smile and concede her quip, when she narrowed her eyes and gazed at me. "Of course, we all know what sport you played. And I do mean 'we.'"

I shut the door a little too loudly behind her.

# 15

I SAT AT MY KITCHEN TABLE FOR A FEW minutes after she left, steaming. What the hell was that all about? How had this case moved so quickly from a run-of-the-mill sex video extortion case to a concussion and the FBI at my door? I needed Cindy Morris like a hole in the head, and in fact I nearly had that anyway, thank you very much.

Now I was even more peeved than after Hamilton called, and had to do something. That turned out to be taking Hopalong to Schiller Park, where we spent most of the time at the casting pond while Hopalong sniffed for carp. I can't say if I felt physically better or worse by the time we got back, but my head, pounding or not, was a little clearer.

The Google pickings were slim on Doug Freeley and American Financial Health Care. The most useful hit was an article in the *Dispatch* a month ago about a lawsuit against the company over some lost investments. It didn't tell me much, but I knew who could fill in the blank spots, assuming there were any. It was 6:30 p.m., but I called the number anyway.

"Kevin Harding, *Dispatch*," he said after one ring.

"It's Andy Hayes," I said. "Can you talk?"

"Sorry, did you want the sports department? Or did your subscription expire again?"

"Har."

"I try."

"Not very hard." I told him why I was calling.

"Doug Freeley," he said. "You're moving up in the world."

"Now why would you say that?"

"Why are you asking about him?"

"Idle curiosity."

"My ass," he said.

Turned out Harding was working a night cops shift, so I invited him to dinner. We met at Dirty Frank's hot dog shop on Fourth Street an hour later. I had a regular dog and one with kimchee on it. Harding's order involved bacon and baked beans.

"Your article about American Financial," I said. "Some kind of lawsuit, right? Don't take this the wrong way, but it was kind of confusing."

"It's the subject matter," he said, taking a bite of his dog. He'd put on a few pounds since the last time I'd seen him, when I was helping him recover some stolen wages for the cousin of his wife, who was from Mexico. He blamed the weight gain on his and Maria's new twins.

"Naturally," I said.

Ignoring me, he said, "American Financial's got a complicated business model. They basically buy up the debt of hospitals and nursing homes and health clinics, anybody waiting on the federal government for Medicaid or Medicare reimbursement."

"OK."

"So," he said. "I'm XYZ Medical Corp. and I'm floating in bills and still have six months before the feds cut me a check. I'm jumping at the opportunity to clean up accounts receivable early. American Financial's more than happy to help."

"How do they make money?"

"Couple ways. They collect program fees from the providers, fee-for-doing-business sort of thing. They also pool the receivables together, secure bonds, sell the bonds to investors, and raise the cash to buy the debt."

"How do the investors make money?"

"Interest on the bonds after they're repaid when American Financial collects the receivables."

I shook my head. "I think you lost me at accounts receivable."

"Told you it was the subject matter. It's hard to wrap your mind around because it's a niche operation that nobody had really figured out a way to make money off of before."

"Do they?"

"What?"

"Make money?"

Harding took another bite and considered. "Why that lawsuit was interesting. Investor claimed he'd lost money. A lot, like a hundred grand."

"Sounds serious."

"Yes and no. Company like American Financial, they do that much in business before the first coffee break. They could argue it was an accounting error, and they might not be totally wrong."

"So why'd you write about it?"

"Slow news day," he said. "Plus there was something about halfway through that caught my eye."

"Oh?"

He reached into the pocket of his sports coat and pulled out a stapled sheaf of papers, folded neatly into thirds. He opened it up, flipped through the pages, then handed it to me. "There, on page 35."

I looked at the paper. Yellow highlighter marked a paragraph. I read, "A good portion of the funding that American Financial secured through the sale of bonds was used to advance money to health care companies without the required purchase of receivables." I looked up at Harding. He nodded, rolled his finger as a signal to keep reading. "American Financial knew that Marymount Dental had no realistic ability to repay the advance it received and lacked adequate receivables to support the amounts it was advanced. Meanwhile, the advances were heavily draining American Financial investment funds. To make up the difference, American Financial sold more bonds."

I looked at Harding. "That must have been one really slow news day."

He grinned. "I know. It's like hieroglyphs. I didn't get it at first. Business desk had to straighten me out. First thing is, you have to cut through the legalese."

"Be my guest."

"This investor is claiming that American Financial's business model was basically rotten. It didn't have the money to buy the debt it was supposed to be purchasing, so it sold more bonds to make up the difference. It sounds complicated, but there's only one expression for an operation that collects money from one place to make up its promises somewhere else. And it doesn't matter how fancy the office is or how many accountants you've got working for you."

I thought about it for a second. Then it dawned on me. "Ponzi scheme."

"Elementary, my dear Andy. You believe what this lawsuit is saying, American Financial's nothing more than a house of cards. A model like that can never sustain itself and the only winners are the guys funneling the cash."

"Guys like Doug Freeley."

"Right."

"So, is it? A Ponzi scheme?"

"That's the big question," he said. "Lawsuit's just one investor, and it's the only one of its kind I've been able to find."

"Any, I don't know, public filings? That kind of thing?"

He shook his head. "Company is privately held, so the Securities and Exchange Commission doesn't get involved. Their lawyer basically told me to perform an unnatural act on myself. And I'm hearing this guy might settle, so that'll shut the door on a trial or anything that might shed some light on this stuff."

"Too bad."

Harding shrugged. "Too bad for my business, maybe. But the investor probably cares more about getting his money back than exposing a corrupt financial scheme. Hard to blame him."

"What do you think? Corrupt or not?"

"I think it's interesting. That's why I wrote about it. Ponzi scheme's a serious charge. On the other hand, the success of their lawsuit doesn't depend on whether it's an old-fashioned shell game or if American Financial is laundering drug money or all the executives beat their wives. Or husbands. That's stuff for the feds, if they got involved. That happens, it's a bigger story. In the meantime, all the lawsuit says is this guy's owed a ton of money and he wants what's coming to him."

I thought about Special Agent Cindy Morris. I knew this was the part of the conversation where I was supposed to trade information with Harding. He'd told me a lot. And here I was sitting on an extremely fat tip. Dropping that piece of information *sotto voce* over a clandestine hot dog dinner was just the kind of thing that was supposed to happen in these circumstances. And I knew it could permanently endear me to Harding, not a small thing given what he seemed to know about pretty much anything nefarious in the city.

But my instincts were flashing red right at the moment. I couldn't explain why, but somehow I knew was it was too early to give up the FBI, despite Morris's crack about the sport I played.

Instead, I said, "Well, are they?"

"Are they what?"

"Are the feds involved?"

"Precisely," Harding said.

"Precisely what?"

"Precisely what I'm trying to find out."

# 16

THE NEXT MORNING I FIELDED CALLS FROM
Ted Hamilton and Doug Freeley, both looking for information.
I also got an e-mail from Cindy Morris. "Anything new?" the
subject line said.

"Odds improving for the Michigan game," I wrote back.
She didn't reply.

HENRY AND HONEY HUNTINGTON lived in Bex-
ley, the first suburb east of the city, a land of big, well-kept
homes and even bigger, well-kept mansions, including one occupied by the governor of the state, another by the president
of Ohio State, and yet another, years ago—much to the city's
consternation—by Larry Flynt, the publisher of *Hustler* magazine. The Huntington residence, on a leafy street off Drexel
Avenue, was somewhere between home and mansion, a pile of
gray stone with a slate roof that seemed the perfect place for a
college professor slash provost, his wife, and two standard poodles named Roger and Hester. It was noon on the nose when I

turned onto their street and cruised slowly past the house. For a moment I worried I'd missed Honey's departure. But two minutes later, as I watched in my rearview mirror, a sporty red BMW backed out of the driveway, maneuvered carefully into the street, then drove off at a not unreasonable rate of speed. If she was having an affair, Honey Huntington was in no hurry to get there. I waited three beats, then pulled out and started the tail. I'm hardly the best in the world at this part of my job, but it wasn't going to be hard to lose track of a red BMW, even in a town obsessed with all things scarlet. And you'd be surprised how invisible an older-model Honda Odyssey van is. One of the reasons I chose it.

We drove west on Broad Street, passing the Columbus School for Girls campus on the left and not too much farther down the grounds of St. Charles Preparatory Academy on the right. We kept going west, into the downtown area, past Broad Street Presbyterian, over the highway, past State Auto and the art museum. We were just passing First Congregational Church when she abruptly turned right onto Cleveland Avenue.

A few minutes later, after a few more turns, I followed her into the parking lot at North Market, the city's 150-year-old destination for anything from locally raised meat and real Indian food to Jeni's original ice cream stand. As awful as I felt physically, this job was starting to look up. Honey wasn't hard to spot as she got out of her car, glanced casually around— perhaps a bit guiltily, I thought—and then strolled toward the market entrance. She was wearing a light red coat with a fur-lined hood and wide red leather belt and a snazzy black felt hat tipped to the left that didn't exactly disguise her presence. Beneath her hat a gorgeous and thick mane of well-coiffed hair the color of, well, honey framed a strikingly beautiful face. For the first time I found myself thinking why her husband might be worried.

Assembling my usual disguise—sunglasses, Columbus Clippers baseball cap, and a winter coat I'd pulled out of the donation bin at Roy's church—I limped after her and kept up as best I could as she briskly marched down the aisles. She had a spring to her step that I'd seen before. She sped past The Fish Guys, turned the corner at the cheese stand, and walked into the waiting embrace of . . . another woman. Dressed as elegantly as herself. Someone with whom she was soon laughing and chatting and sharing photographs from her phone and generally leaving the impression of a girl-friends' day out.

They ordered takeout at the Indian stand and took it to one of the tables upstairs. I sat with my own Vietnamese pho a few tables over. I didn't dare sit close enough to eavesdrop with confidence, but in any case the tawdriest phrase I heard float from their table involved cleaning up dog crap. After lunch, they left the market and made their way on foot past the Greek Orthodox Cathedral up to High Street, and as I followed in painful pursuit they strolled through the Short North neighborhood, splitting their time between window-shopping and actual excursions inside the numerous jewelry, card, clothing, antique, and bric-a-brac stores crowding both sides of the street. The last stop turned out to be a store called Banninger's Buttons, where they entered and stayed. And stayed. There's only so much you can do in the Short North in the middle of the day, and only so many places a big guy like myself can hide, and there are very few button shops where I wouldn't stand out like a bull in a Precious Moments store. In the end I went over to the bus stop across the street and sat, keeping an eye on the shop door. Finally, al-most forty-five minutes later, Honey emerged, alone, a Ban-ninger's Buttons bag in her hand.

She walked back to the North Market, got into the red BMW, and retraced her route to Bexley. I clocked the round trip at exactly two hours. I watched her go back inside and heard, from the inner recesses of the house, the unmistakable high-pitched tones of a woman greeting her beloved poodles.

I thought about what I'd just seen. Was it possible Honey's affair, if indeed it was such a thing, was a little more complicated than her husband imagined?

ABOUT AN HOUR AFTER I returned home, I got a call from Henry Huntington, wondering how it had gone. I explained what I'd seen, leaving out my suspicions about what might be going on between Honey and her friend. He seemed more put out by my description of the window-shopping than I thought necessary, but he thanked me and told me to continue my good work. I resisted the temptation to respond with an "Aye-aye" and tried unsuccessfully to figure out why he bugged me so much.

At five o'clock that afternoon I picked up my son Mike at his mom's house in Worthington, a suburb just north of Columbus with a distinctly New England character thanks to the early settlers who founded it after pushing west from Connecticut and Massachusetts. Mike lived in a plain vanilla split-level ranch around the corner from the downtown, but there were clapboard houses close to the main drag that wouldn't have looked out of place in older parts of Boston or Providence. From there I drove farther up the road to Powell, a village turned booming upscale suburb that had successfully siphoned off a lot of residents fleeing the problems of Columbus in recent years, and got my other son, Joe, at *his* mom's house. It was a rare aligning of my custody arrangement stars, and I intended to take full advantage of it. We were bound for a Columbus Blue Jackets hockey game at Nationwide Arena just north of downtown, a sprawling office and apartment re-development on the site of the old Ohio State Penitentiary. We parked in a lot opposite the old Union Station arch, the only thing saved when Columbus's train station was demolished in the 1970s. If nothing else, Columbus was good at getting rid of history. Sometimes I liked it that way.

"Gonna be a good game," I said as we settled into our seats. We were all juggling the requisite hot dogs and fries and pop. "Jackets have won three straight." Despite the missing laptop, my encounter in the alley two nights before, the headache that wouldn't go away, and the fact that I was still having trouble bending my left knee, I finally felt like I could relax a bit.

"I hope there's a fight tonight," said Joe, who was eight.

"There's always a fight," said Mike, two years older, trying to sound like he'd seen it all when it came to hockey fights. Joe wasn't fooled.

"How do you know? You've only been to one game."

Mike shook his head. "Nuh uh. Three, four. Maybe more."

"Have not."

"Have too."

"When?" said Joe, who like his mother was not one to let an issue drop. "When have you seen another game?"

"Lots of times. Dad took me."

"Is that true?" Joe said, looking at me with a fierce glance of betrayal.

"Not *him*," Mike said. "Steve, I mean. He's got season tickets."

Steve. His stepdad. Though that's not how he'd referred to him.

"It's not a contest, guys," I said weakly.

"I wish you had season tickets," Joe said.

"Well," I said, fanning out the stubs from our three tickets. "I have these. And it's the season. Does that count?"

"I guess," Joe said.

"Maybe we can go next week," I said, instantly regretting it, since I knew I didn't have the money budgeted for another game.

"You don't have us next week," Mike said. "You don't have us until a week from this weekend."

"Right," I said. "Well, a week from this weekend, then."

"That's Joe's Cub Scout weekend," Mike said.

I stared at him. "It is?"

"Yeah."

"How do you know that?"

"I just do."

I started thinking how pathetic it was that Mike knew more about the schedule of a half brother he didn't live with than I did, and that got me reflecting on my faults in the parenthood department, a path I knew from experience I really didn't want to go down, when mercifully my cell phone went off.

Though in hindsight, maybe not so mercifully.

"Hayes?" A male voice.

"That's me."

"Detective Fielding, Columbus Police Department."

"Long time no talk to," I said.

"Need a couple minutes of your time."

"I'm a little busy at the moment."

"What a coincidence. So am I. How soon can you be downtown?"

"Not soon," I said, skirting the fact that I was already more or less downtown. "Mind if I ask what this is about?"

"You know somebody named Danny Reilly?"

I paused. "No. Should I?"

"How's eight o'clock sound?"

I looked at my watch. It was just past seven. The crowd had roared its approval for the Blue Jackets' regular National Anthem crooner, a baritone named Leo, and the Jackets and the Colorado Avalanche were lining up for the first drop of the puck.

"It doesn't sound good. I've got my boys with me right now, and—"

"I can always send someone for you," he said. "If that would help."

"It wouldn't. What's so urgent it can't wait until morning?"

"Plenty."

"Anything you can share over the phone?"

"Nothing. What'll it be? Eight o'clock, or uniformed pickup?"

"This is really inconvenient."

"I bet it is."

"All right," I said. "I'll be there as soon as I can. I've got to take my boys home first. That's going to take a little while."

"Sorry for the trouble. Ask for me at the front desk." And he hung up.

I looked blankly at the ice. A Jackets player from Russia threaded his way past the Avalanche and flicked the puck toward the net, stymied only by a brilliant goal save.

"What's the matter?" Mike said. Always the perceptive one. The kid who knew his half brother's Cub Scout schedule.

"We have to go. Something's come up. I'm really sorry."

"Go where?" Joe said.

"Go home. Your home, I mean."

"Why?"

"It's, ah, business-related."

"Now?" Mike said with the incredulousness of an adult.

"I'm really sorry," I said.

"The game just started!" Joe wailed.

"I'm sorry," I repeated.

We struggled out of our seats and headed for the exit.

Joe said, "This always happens."

I said, "What?"

"We can never do stuff with you. You always get interrupted."

I couldn't immediately think of anything to say.

"He's right," Mike said. "It's always something."

Then he reached down, grabbed Joe's hand, and they walked ahead of me, together, down the corridor, snaking their way past late fans rushing to get into the arena.

# 17

A COUPLE OF DECADES AGO, BACK WHEN I had other things on my mind, Columbus commissioned the creation of a full-scale replica of the *Santa Maria*, the flagship of Christopher Columbus, as part of a five-hundredth anniversary celebration of the New World's "discovery." The ship was anchored on the banks of the Scioto River downtown, where it still sits, visited daily by joggers accessing the local fitness trail, schoolchildren bused in from the suburbs, and authentic city center homeless people. It floats just across from the federal courthouse and kitty-corner, sort of, from the Columbus police station. There are days when I look at the ship and it makes me think of the promise of new horizons. And then there were nights like tonight, when it reminded me of a miniature slave galley.

Fierce-looking concrete lions used to guard the police station's entrance off Marconi Street, and I would have welcomed the chance to return their scowl, given my mood. It was nearly 9 p.m. Fielding had called my phone half an hour earlier but I'd let it ring, being in the middle of the second verbal drubbing from an ex-wife that night. The uniformed cop at the high desk in the center of the station lobby heard me out and told me to wait while he made a call. Fielding was down a few minutes later and accompanied me up to the sixth floor without speaking. Once there, we walked back into the warren of homicide offices. Fielding led me into an interview room, shut the door, and sat down opposite me. The air inside was stale and smelled of sweat—not of athletic endeavor, but the perspiration that comes from fear, and bluster, and despair.

"Danny Reilly," Fielding said. "You sure you don't know him?"

"Sure."

"We pulled Reilly out of Grandview Yard quarry this afternoon. Fisherman snagged him."

I said, "OK."

"Reilly had a cell phone in his pocket. A little waterlogged, but we've got the best techs around. Want to guess what they found on it?"

I shook my head. I had a feeling I already knew.

"Your picture. Your photo, I should say. Time stamped within the half hour of when you said you were mugged."

I didn't say anything.

"I don't recall you mentioning the guy took your picture."

"Memory was a little sketchy," I said. "Baseball bats will do that."

"He also had a tattoo of Ohio Stadium on his neck. That slip your mind too?"

"It was dark."

"Too dark to notice a tattoo of the 'Shoe'?"

"You know how it is. Any sign of my ring?"

"No."

"Too bad."

"Wouldn't have thought you cared," Fielding said.

"I like to surprise people."

"Reilly was shot. Any thoughts on that?"

"Where?"

"In the body."

"Thank you."

"Well?"

"I don't know who he is and I didn't shoot him. How's that?"

"Where were you last night?"

"Went out to dinner. Home by 8 p.m."

"With who?"

"With a friend."

Fielding sighed. "You're not helping."

"Neither are you. So quit pussyfooting around. You think I had something to do with this."

"I'm not thinking anything, other than you left a bunch of stuff out the other night. And you wouldn't be the first person who got roughed up by somebody and took matters into your own hands."

"And how many of those people left incriminating cell phones in their victims' pockets? Or am I trying to 'plant' evidence to deter suspicion?" I made air quotes around "plant," which I could tell annoyed him.

"You done?"

"I'm done suggesting the plot of every bad TV cop drama I've seen in the past twenty years, yes."

"Is that right?"

"Yes," I said. "That's right."

"So you have no idea who this guy is, why he wanted to tangle with you, and how he ended up in the middle of a quarry with a bullet in him?"

"None."

Fielding looked at me, then looked at the wall. Then back. I said, "Are we done here?"

"I don't know. Are we?"

"Am I a suspect?"

"Have I read you your rights?"

"Then I can go."

"You go when I say you can."

"Look," I said, sitting back. "I want to help you. I'm not trying to be obtuse. But I really don't know anything about this guy. I'm sorry I forgot to mention the cell phone. Past two days I've woken up with those little cartoon birdies circling my head. He beat the shit out of me, I'm not ashamed to say."

Fielding didn't respond. He looked at me for a long minute, then produced a blank police statement form and pushed it across the table.

"Write down the details from the other night. In the alley."

"I already did that. In the hospital."

"Do it again, and don't leave anything out this time. And then write down what you just told me. About not knowing Danny Reilly. And then make sure we have every way known to man to reach you. Not planning any out-of-town trips in the near future, are you?"

"It's tempting," I said. "But no."

"Don't be a stranger," Fielding said, and stood up and walked out of the room.

As I stared blankly at the paper in front of me, my phone buzzed. I looked down. It was an automatic text alert I'd signed up for with the local NBC affiliate.

"Breaking News," it read. "Blue Jackets win in overtime."

# 18

I LAY IN BED THE NEXT MORNING TRYING
to decide which had been worse, the third-degree I'd gotten
from Fielding or the tongue lashing from my exes. Then I realized that neither experience was a fraction as bad as the look on
my sons' faces when I'd told them we had to leave the game.
And with that I got slowly and painfully up.

I had made it through the morning rituals of coffee, shower,
and walking the dog when Burke called. It was 8:01 a.m. Not a
good sign.

"Any chance you could come by the office?"

"Now?" I said, realizing immediately how stupid that
sounded.

"That would be the general idea," he said in an even voice.
"Everything OK?"

"Eight-thirty sound good?"

Based on his tone I agreed that eight-thirty sounded not
just good but perfect. Despite aches and pains almost everywhere, I was dressed, out the door, and in the car ten minutes
later and at his office with two minutes to spare.

"Morning," Burke's secretary said as I hurried inside.

"LaTasha," I said, nodding distractedly.

She showed no surprise at seeing me, and nor did I expect any. LaTasha usually knew what Burke was doing a few minutes before he did.

Burke's Front Street office had a bank of windows that looked out on an office courtyard, which in the warm weather practically glowed with redbud and magnolia trees. Beyond it you could just see a glint of the Scioto River. His walls had the requisite college and law school diplomas, but those were dwarfed by pictures of his wife and children and extended family.

"Morning," he said as I walked in.

"Morning," I responded.

As soon as I sat down LaTasha entered the room with a tray of coffee, cream, sugar, and what I knew were some of Dorothy's homemade muffins. No chipped Garfield mugs and plastic cutlery for Burke. He served his coffee, which he blissfully never asked if you cared for first, in real china. Burke got up, poured a cup for me, then for himself, then sat back down at his desk.

"I had a visitor yesterday," he said. "FBI Special Agent Cynthia Morris."

I waited. It had not been a question.

"She's concerned that you've been speaking to someone named Doug Freeley."

I took a sip of coffee and continued waiting.

"It was an unusual visit in that Freeley hasn't been charged with a crime and I haven't been asked to represent him. Nor," he added, with what could have been a hint of displeasure, "does it appear that I ever will."

I took another, bigger sip. I knew Burke bought his coffee beans fresh from Stauf's in Grandview, and you could tell. It was the best-tasting cup of coffee I'd had since the last time I was in his office undergoing a similar conversation.

"Morris was here was because she knows you work for me. That and the fact she and I go back a few years, and have shared the same courtroom on a number of occasions. We're not friends, of course."

I nodded.

"Anyway," Burke said, "I thought you might find that interesting. You have your own business, and you're under no obligation to tell me what you do on that side of things. Except, I'm going to suggest, when FBI agents pay me a visit."

Just as I'd known that Burke's earlier comments had not been questions, I knew that his last statement had been an invitation.

I started with Ted Hamilton and our conversation at Cup o' Joe. It took me about ten minutes to get all the way through, ending with Danny Reilly's body and the events of the evening before with Detective Fielding at the police station.

"I told Hamilton to call you," Burke said.

"That's right."

"And a week later the FBI's on my doorstep and you're a suspect in a murder."

"Person of interest," I said. "Twice removed."

"I do know how to pick them, don't I?" Burke said.

"HERE'S THE THING," Burke said. He was standing now, looking out his window, coffee cup in hand. He'd taken a bite of muffin, which had been the signal for me to indulge as well, and although I hadn't felt hungry when I walked into his office, I realized I was famished. The tension was easing from the room as Burke talked, as it always did.

He said, "The FBI's interested in Freeley. It's got something to do with his company. I'm guessing the books are cooked."

"That would be my guess too," I said.

"Those files, on the laptop. Probably something about the business he didn't want anyone to see."

"Probably."

"Any idea what they were?"

"Rows and rows of numbers on some spreadsheets. Beyond that, not a clue. It was gone before I had a chance to explore."

"No idea, besides Hamilton or Freeley, who would want the laptop badly enough to go after you and then, for some reason, this Danny Reilly?"

"None."

Burke folded his hands, a sign I knew from experience meant our interview was almost over.

"You're in some deep waters here," he said. "I could count on one hand the number of times the FBI has come to see me like that and still have enough digits left to give them the finger. And if that weren't bad enough, there's this business with Reilly."

"Right," I said.

"On the other hand, as much as I hate to say it, the robbery may have inadvertently solved the problem. I'm sure the fact the laptop is missing is no consolation to Hamilton, or Freeley. But the fact is, it's gone. There's not a whole lot left to do right now. Except wait. And maybe hope it stays missing."

"Right," I said again.

"And that is what you're planning to do, correct?"

I looked at him.

"Wait?" he said. "Not make any more moves?"

I shrugged. "What else can I do?"

"Good answer."

I added, perhaps too quickly, "Although I wouldn't mind moving out of the crosshairs for Reilly."

"I wouldn't mind that either. I've got a list of things I'm going to need you to do soon, and this is not a distraction I'm interested in. Let's just wait and see what happens. Your mugging and Reilly's death are a hell of a coincidence. But still a coincidence. Fielding's a smart guy. He'll figure that out sooner rather than later. But in the meantime, try to stay out of trouble."

I nodded, and seeing that he had sat down at his desk, I stood.

"Thanks for coming by so early," he said.

"Thanks for the coffee," I replied.

We shook hands and I was on my way.

"Have a nice day," LaTasha said brightly as I emerged from Burke's office and passed into the lobby.

"On my to-do list," I said.

I kept a low profile for the rest of the day. Took the van in for an oil change. Gave Hopalong a long-overdue bath. Sweated over some billing issues. Practiced snapping cell phone pictures in the backyard, trying to improve my ability to nail the money shot, but managed only two clear photos of a pair of amorous squirrels. Exhausted by my exertions, in the late afternoon I walked down to the Hey Hey Bar & Grill on Whittier Street, the bar so nice they named it twice, and ate sauerkraut balls washed down with a couple of glasses of draft Yuengling. And then a couple more. And then I went home, stretched out on the couch, picked up my Steve Jobs biography, read two chapters, and decided to rest my eyes. It was a long rest.

BETWEEN THE GRILLING I'D gotten from Fielding Wednesday night and the one Burke handed out on Thursday, the last way I wanted to spend Friday was trailing Honey Huntington through the Short North again. But I needed money more than sympathy, and so I made sure I was in place by noon, just like her husband required. The next two hours unfolded almost exactly as they had on Wednesday, except that she and her companion dined at Northstar Café before heading into Banninger's Buttons.

Eventually, after I saw Honey safely back to Bexley and the delighted barks of Roger and Hester, I drove around the corner and up a couple of side streets until I got to Main. I parked, went into Rubino's Pizza, sat down and ordered a thin-crust pepperoni pizza. I checked my e-mail on my phone while I waited, then, because the restaurant wasn't all that full midafternoon and I didn't need to worry about offending my fellow diners, called Kevin Harding at the *Dispatch* on a lark and asked him about Ted Hamilton.

"First Doug Freeley, now a Statehouse lobbyist," Harding said. "Any connection?"

"They both appear to be assholes. Beyond that, no idea."

"So as usual, you don't know anything."

"I know enough to call you when I want information," I said. "And that's the only buttering up you're going to get."

"So what do you need to know?"

It was a good question. *Just ask a few of his associates if they think he'd be up to killing someone who had video evidence of him trying to seduce a barely overage girl. Hypothetically, of course.*

Instead, I said, "I just need some background on him. The kind of stuff I won't find by Googling him or scrolling through your archives."

"Sounds only semi-intriguing. Is there a story in it?"

"I sure hope not," I said. "But you're at the top of my list if one magically appears."

"I'm sure I am," he said. "I'll get back to you."

"Thanks," I said. "Best to Maria. And the twins."

"They don't talk yet," Harding said. "But whatever." And hung up.

# 19

WHEN I WOKE UP ON SATURDAY, I KNEW
exactly what I needed to do, despite Burke's warnings otherwise. And it didn't involve hunkering down in front of the TV
for the Ohio State–Wisconsin game in Madison.

I'd like to say that finding out where the late great Danny
Reilly had lived had taken some shoe leather, but it was as simple as reading the address in the short story the *Dispatch* did
on the discovery of his body. The rundown rental complex off
State Route 161 looked about right for what I knew of the guy.
It was a part of town that had seen its glory days in the sixties and seventies when subdivisions crept away from the city
core but stayed in Columbus proper, thanks to annexation. A
glut of apartment buildings accompanied by rag-tag crime had
brought property values down considerably since then. An in-
fusion of small businesses run by the city's burgeoning Somali
and Mexican populations offered some promise, but salvation
was still several stimulus packages away. I pulled a plastic bag
full of advertising inserts off the door handle at Reilly's address
and rang the bell.

A dark-complected woman answered the door. Late twenties, maybe thirties. She was wearing flip-flops despite the chill in the air, faded jeans a little too tight, and an Ohio State hoodie. She had one of those handwritten tattoos across her neck, and it was both hard to miss on its own and hard to miss because it said "Jimmy," not "Danny." The other thing that was hard to miss was the bruise under her left eye, which unless I was mistaken did not come from accidentally running into a doorknob.

"Yeah," she said.

"Andy Hayes," I said, and handed her my card.

She stared at it. "Private investigator," she said, after a minute. "Like Sherlock Holmes, huh?"

"He was a consulting detective, actually," I said.

"What?"

"Never mind. Could I come in?"

"The police have already been here. I told them everything I knew."

"I'm not the police."

"Like I care. What do you want?"

"You know Danny Reilly?"

"Knew him."

"Sorry for your loss."

"Not a big deal."

I hesitated. "Danny took something of mine. I need it back."

"You knew him?"

"I'm the guy he beat up a few hours before he was killed."

HER NAME WAS MARY MILLER. We sat on her couch; like everything else in the apartment, which smelled of fried food and cigarettes, it looked like a secondhand store reject. She muted the home makeover show she'd been watching.

"I don't know anything about Danny and you," she said. "That stuff was all strictly his deal."

"That stuff?"

"The Night Shift. That's what he called it. Stuff he did after work, that is, when he was working. He didn't tell me and I didn't ask."

*I bet you asked at least once,* I said to myself, looking at her bruised eye.

"Fine by me," I said. "That's not why I'm here. Well, sort of not why I'm here."

"Then sort of why are you?"

"Danny took a laptop I had. I need it back. I'm also curious why he took it."

"Don't know nothing about a laptop."

"You didn't see him with it, that night?"

"Like I said, Night Shift was off limits. I told him to be careful. He never listened."

"He didn't say if somebody asked him to take it from me?" She shook her head.

I decided to change course. "You said he worked?"

"Sometimes. Construction mostly. When they would take him on."

"You know where?"

"All over. He never told me where he was going."

"Do you know who he worked for?"

"Couple different companies. A lot of times he'd just get a call the night before."

"You remember the names of the companies?"

She shook her head again. She was starting to look bored. I changed course again.

"Do you know if Danny was from here? Did he have any family?"

"He wasn't from Columbus, I know that," she said.

"Do you know where?"

"Some place south. Smaller. He was always complaining about Columbus. Said it made him feel squeezed in. He hated all the traffic."

"Some place south. Like Texas? Florida?"

"Some place south in *Ohio*. Hell, I don't know if he'd even been out of the state. I tried to talk him into going to Atlanta once, to see my cousins. He hated the idea."

"Southern Ohio. Do you know where?"

"Sorry," she said. "Danny wasn't a big talker, if you know what I mean."

I thought back to the string of expletives he'd unleashed on me the night of the attack.

"And no idea why he wanted to steal my laptop?"

"Nope," she said, as though it were the dumbest question she'd heard all day. Which it might have been.

I said, "So he worked for a company that you don't know, in places around Columbus that you don't know, and he was from a small town that you don't know. Anything else about Danny you don't know that might be helpful?"

She stared at me. "You getting wise with me?"

"I'm just trying to get some answers. Maybe even find out something that will help figure out who did this to Danny."

"Why do you care? You said he beat you up."

"I hate mysteries," I said. "Mind if I ask you another question?"

She shook her head. Her eyes had drifted to the TV.

"Who gave you that shiner?"

Her hand moved involuntarily toward the bruised area, but stopped short of touching it. As she raised her arm I noticed another bruise, faint but still mottled.

"I tripped," she said.

"On what? Danny's fist?"

"Fuck you. You should leave."

"Why'd you stay with him?"

"I said you should leave."

"What's the big hurry? Expecting company?"

"Get the fuck out."

I stood up, placing a card on the table in front of me. She watched me move but didn't say anything. I was at the door and opening it when I heard my name. I looked back and she was holding my card.

"He owed me three hundred bucks in rent money. So I'm short this month."

"I'm sorry about that."

"Not as sorry as me."

"Call me if you think of anything else," I said.

"Probably won't. But will if I do," she said, and she suddenly sounded much younger. I tried to think of something to add, but Mary Miller had already gone back to watching TV. I stepped outside and pulled the door shut behind me. I noticed that at some point there had been hinges for a screen door, but that had been a long time ago. Long before Danny and Mary lived here.

I PULLED INTO THE cramped parking lot of Carfagna's Italian grocery store a few minutes later. I told myself I had been in that neck of the woods anyway. Making lemonade from lemons. Something like that.

I went inside, walked to the rear to the butcher's and took a red ticket from the number counter. No. 23. I went back up the aisle and browsed the wine section for ten minutes. I settled on a Côtes du Rhône marked off $3. I grabbed a little red cart, pushed it around the corner, selected three quart jars of Carfagna's puttanesca sauce and four twenty-eight-ounce cans of diced tomatoes, then went back to the butcher's counter and waited. I watched as a woman who bore a passing resemblance to a younger Sophia Loren bought two standing rib roasts, a rack of ribs, and three whole chickens. I was admiring the sweater she had on and was wondering what she wore when she cooked and had just checked out whether she had a wedding band—she did, and next to it a rock that must have cost several standing rib roasts and then some—when they called my number. I pulled myself together and bought ten pounds of garlic roasted sausage and two pork roasts.

I had pulled back onto Dublin-Granville Road and was sitting at a light behind a car with an "I Bleed Scarlet and Gray" bumper sticker when I realized I hadn't asked Mary Miller if she knew anything about my Big Ten ring. I don't know why, or if, I wanted it back. I couldn't explain why, after everything, I still wore it. But all of a sudden I knew that I had to know one way or the other.

As I pulled back into the parking lot, the first thing I noticed was that the space I'd parked in before was occupied by a newish Nissan SUV, bright red. The second thing I saw was that two big guys, one white, one black, were pushing their way into Mary's apartment. They were both wearing gray Buckeye hoodies. Just like the two guys that my neighbor saw running out of my house.

I knew what I had to do, but I hesitated nonetheless. I was still moving slowly from my encounter with Reilly, barely beyond the shuffle I needed to keep up with Honey Huntington. Since I can't carry a gun, the closest thing I have for protection is the baseball bat that was so useful in self-defense the other night. I thought about dialing Roy, but even assuming I could reach him, it would take him twenty minutes plus to get here.

So no choice. I did what I always do. I grabbed the bat and blundered ahead.

MARY WAS IN HER recliner on the far side of the living room, rubbing the right side of her face, when I limped in. A trickle of blood ran down from the corner of her mouth. One of the guys, the black one, was standing at the alcove entrance to the kitchen, arms folded. The other guy was looming over Mary. Both had gloves on. They had complemented their hoodies with workout pants and basketball shoes.

I cleared my throat. I said, "Breaking and entering, *and* hitting a woman. How chivalrous of you."

Both men turned and stared.

"What the fuck are you doing here?" the white guy said.

"Guess I could ask you the same," I said.

"Get the fuck out," the black guy said.

"I don't think so," I said.

"You don't think shit," the white guy said, starting to come toward me.

I pulled the baseball bat from behind my back with my right hand and palmed the thick end in my left. The white guy paused, and in that moment I did something that surprised me. I said to him, "Now hold on a second, Freddie."

He stopped and stared at me again. I didn't blame him. His name had come to me out of the blue, like an unexpected slice of pie pushed across the counter at a diner. Freddie Carmichael. Ohio State defensive lineman four, maybe five seasons back. Heavily recruited, middling college career. Never graduated.

I looked at the other guy. "Darryl," I said. "Darryl Nysong." Same story, I recalled. Another lineman. Big, very big. Both of them. I'm over two hundred, barely, and they both outweighed me by a couple of footlockers.

"How the fuck do you know my name?" Darryl said.

"I have a photographic memory," I said. "I recall all the big-time Ohio State losers."

"Asshole," Freddie said. "Time for you to leave."

Freddie moved fast for a big guy, but then he was a good fifteen years younger than me. I moved not so fast on my better days and pretty slowly when I'm still recovering from a beating. I took an awkward step back to brace for his charge but almost immediately felt my left knee buckle. He was on me before I could begin to raise the bat, and before I knew it he'd wrestled it from my arms and slammed me against the wall. *Not again,* I thought. I caught a glimpse of Mary getting up from the chair and running from the room, and then the first blow came, a practiced jab to the gut with the thick end of the bat, followed by his fist on my jaw, after which I sagged slowly down the wall. I had just enough sense to raise both hands to ward off the next swing of the bat, and then before I really knew what had happened Freddie Carmichael was straddling me and the second punch came, and lots of things flashed in front of me. I felt rather than heard Darryl come from behind, grab my arms, and pull them back, hard. I let out an involuntary gasp of pain.

"You don't belong here," Freddie said, and punched me hard a third time.

"Go to hell," I managed, trying to struggle, but it was hopeless and I knew it. It was like trying to budge a pair of refrigerators.

I was bracing for the next blow when I heard a sound behind me that seemed familiar yet I couldn't quite place. I looked up and saw Freddie frozen, his right arm poised almost comically in space.

"Get off him," Mary said. I craned my head up. She was standing at the end of the hall, a shotgun in her arms. The sound I'd heard had been her racking a shell into the chamber.

"What the fuck," Darryl said, but I noticed he wasn't moving much either. I pulled my arms free, ignoring the pain, and carefully, slowly, swaying a bit, stood up. I backed away, down the hall.

"Fuck you, bitch," Freddie said. "Like you'd actually use that thing."

"Let's find out," Mary said. "This apartment's due for a deep cleaning."

"OK," Darryl said. "Nice and easy. Why don't you put it down and we'll just talk some more."

"Get out," Mary said. "Now."

"Wait," I said.

They all looked at me.

"What were they here for?" I said.

"Here?" Mary said.

"Why are they here? What are they looking for?"

Without changing her stance, the shotgun still leveled at Freddie, she said, "Same as you, shithead. The laptop. I thought you'd sent them in after you left."

"Not me," I said.

"I figured as much after he clocked you and you went down like a girl."

"Thanks," I said. I turned to stare at Freddie. "Why are you after this laptop?"

"Fuck you," he said.

"Here's what I'm thinking," I said. "You guys broke into my house, ransacked it, looking for the computer. Then Danny Reilly came along and got it instead. What he didn't know is you were waiting around and saw him. Tried to take it back—maybe put a bullet in his stomach and pushed him into the quarry when he wouldn't cooperate. They still have the death penalty in this state, you know. Even for one douche bag killing another."

"Fuck you," Freddie said once again, but he didn't sound so sure. "We didn't fucking kill anyone."

"That's what they all say," I said. I turned to Darryl. "How about you? Danny mouth off and you decide to clip him?"

"The hell I did," he said, his eyes not on me but on Mary.

"Guess we'll let the jury sort that one out," I said. "So back to my original question: why are you here?"

Neither of them said anything. I continued, "You must have tracked Danny here somehow. Why? Who sent you?"

"Fuck you," Freddie said.

I looked up, and Mary and I exchanged the briefest of glances.

She moved forward and pressed the barrel of the gun against Freddie's back. He shuddered involuntarily.

"Who?" I said.

Darryl said, "Just tell him."

"Shut up," Freddie said.

"Like it's worth any of this," Darryl said. "Come on."

Mary pushed the barrel into Freddie's back firmly enough that he had to inch forward.

"Fuck you," Freddie said. "It was Bobby Fletcher."

I stared at him. "Bobby Fletcher?"

"Bobby sent us, OK?" Darryl said, sounding almost miffed. "Swear to God. Now how about you let us just walk out of here and everything's good."

I glanced at Mary. She gave an almost imperceptible nod. I hobbled into the kitchen to give them room to pass.

"All right," I said. "Get out."

I waited as they went through the door, and I kept it open as I watched them walk down the sidewalk and over to their Nissan. Then I watched as Freddie paused, walked over to my van, took the bat, *my* bat, and swung it hard, knocking a long crack in my windshield with his first blow, then spiderwebbing it with the second. Freddie looked back toward me, gave me the finger, then got into the Nissan, where Darryl was already inside, engine running. They pulled away with the requisite gunning of engine and spitting of parking lot dust and gravel.

As soon as I was sure they were gone, I turned around, walked back in, shut the door and shot the bolt. I hobbled back down the entrance hall. Mary raised the gun and pointed it right at my chest.

"Who the fuck," she said, "is Bobby Fletcher?"

# 20

"FIRST OFF," I SAID, SLOWLY. "THANK YOU."

"For what?"

"For saving my ass."

"How do you know their names?" she demanded, "if they're not with you?"

"I know more about Ohio State football than I thought I did."

"Big fucking coincidence, if you ask me," she said. "You're here, you leave, they come in, you know their names."

"Fair enough," I said. "Except for the part about them beating me up."

"What about this Fletcher guy. Who is he?"

"Happy to tell you," I said. "But maybe not at gunpoint?"

She looked hard at me, then beyond me to the door, then back. Slowly she lowered the gun.

"All right," she said. "Explain. But no funny business."

"Wouldn't think of it," I said, as I found myself slowly sliding down the wall again. "Promise."

"BOBBY FLETCHER," I SAID, a few minutes later. I was sitting on her couch holding an Ohio State mug filled with water and hoping the four aspirin she'd scrounged from her medicine cabinet would work sooner rather than later.

"Waiting," she said. She had a bag of frozen peas on her right cheek.

"He's like a super Ohio State fan," I started.

"Who isn't around here?"

"This is different. He's got this RV, the Band Wagon. He's famous for it. Totally decked out in OSU stuff. Over the top."

"They all are."

"Not like this," I said. "Trust me. But that's not all. He used to be a big-time booster, back when you could do that kind of thing. Back in my day."

"Your day?"

"When I played, I mean."

"You played at Ohio State?"

I nodded. "Yeah." This was a rare conversation in my experience.

"Go on."

"Time was when guys like Fletcher could actually help recruit players. 'Frontliners,' they called them, way back when. Different names, over time. System's gone, but guys like Fletcher are still around."

"What's he do?"

"Do?"

"For a living," she said impatiently.

"He runs a chain of nursing homes."

"How do you know so much about him?"

"I just do," I said. "Bobby and I go back a ways."

"You and Bobby the super fan go way back, but you don't know anything about the two chumps who said he sent them to break into my apartment. And I'm supposed to believe that?"

"I haven't talked to Bobby in a long time."

"You sure about that?"

"I'm sure."

She stared at the TV, where the home makeover show was still on, the sound muted as an attractive-looking couple perused an empty living room. She adjusted the bag of peas on her cheek.

"This whole thing stinks, you know that?" she said.

"Tell me about it."

"And how come they wanted this laptop too?"

"I wish I knew. You sure you don't have it?"

She hesitated. "Not anymore."

"So you did."

"I guess," she said.

"Why didn't you tell me before?"

"Didn't think it was any of your business."

"Seems like it is now. What happened?"

"Why should I tell you?"

"Maybe because we're even?"

"Even?"

"When I walked in here, Freddie and Darryl were in the middle of messing you up. Possibly you could have gotten to your little friend there"—I nodded at the gun—"or possibly not. Things might have gone not so great. So maybe you could look at it like: I saved your pretty face from further rearranging, after which you saved my ugly mug from another unnecessary demolition project."

She thought about it for a minute. Then, for the first time in our long acquaintanceship, Mary Miller smiled. Barely.

"All right, shithead. Fair enough."

"So," I said. "Laptop."

"Danny brought it back last week. Came back late. Swear to God I don't know where he got it from. If he took it from you I'm sorry. Like I said before, he had his Night Shift stuff and it was better if I didn't ask questions."

"Understood."

"He was up half the night looking at it, pulling up files and shit. I kept asking him what he wanted it for, why he took it, but he wouldn't say anything. Next night he left again, and never came back. And that's the last time I saw him."

"He took the laptop with him that night?"

She shook her head. "Left it in our room."

"Didn't say where he was going?"

"Said he was meeting somebody and things were gonna change after that."

"Did he say who?"

"Nope. Next thing I heard was from the police, knocking on my door."

"You tell them any of this?"

"Shit, no. You think I'm crazy? Back bedroom was piled with stuff he'd stolen. I'm lucky they didn't have a warrant. They tried to look around, but I told them my baby was sleeping."

"Your baby?"

She smiled again. Patted the shotgun.

"Nice," I said. "Yours?"

"Danny's," she said. "But it's mine now."

"Thought it looked familiar," I said, thinking back to my encounter with Reilly in the alley. "How'd you learn to handle it?"

"Picked some things up along the way," she said. "You know."

"OK," I said, not really wanting to know. "So where's the laptop now?"

She hesitated.

I said, "Even Steven. Remember?"

"Danny's stepmom," she said.

"All right," I said. "Why her?"

"I knew I had to get it out of here. Her son's this computer whiz—figured he could do something with it. Figure out those files, why Danny had it."

"Why not just give it to the son?"

She darkened. "Brenda's the only one in that whole fucking family who liked me. Didn't look down on me. She's my friend. Was, I guess."

"Brenda's the stepmom?"

"Brenda Brown, yeah."

"What didn't they like about you?"

"Are you blind?" she said. "Notice the color of my skin?"

"Didn't seem to bother Danny," I said.

"Oh, it bothered him," Mary Miller said. "That's why he shut his eyes whenever he fucked me."

# 21

THERE WERE A LOT OF THINGS I SHOULD have done after that, starting with a trip to see Fletcher. But it was a Saturday, which meant game day, plus Ohio State was away, so there was no telling where Fletcher was or who he'd be with, up to and including Freddie Carmichael and Darryl Nysong. There was the fact I was having even more trouble walking thanks to my second thumping of the week. And then there was the little matter of my windshield, which took almost two hours to fix by the time the glass guys showed up. After all that, it was all I could do just to drive myself back to German Village. Confrontation was not in the books.

I never did ask Mary about my ring.

I had brought in my trophies from Carfagna's and put everything away, let the dog out for a quick tour of the backyard, and was sitting on the couch with a Black Label in hand and the game barely under way on TV when my cell phone went off. Roy.

"I'm starving," he said. "Let's go over to Plank's and eat some pizza and watch the game. Just like old times."

"You mean like two weeks ago? Don't you have souls to save?"

"They're sleeping it off still," he said. "I'll roust everyone later for the Saturday Night Special."

Only Roy Richards, I thought, Iraq war veteran and divinity school graduate, would name his evening church service after a cheap handgun.

"Tell you what," I said, and explained how my morning had gone.

"Sheesh," he said when I'd finished. "Guess we'll eat in."

I OPENED MY EYES the next morning, Sunday, and stared at my living room ceiling for several minutes, trying to put together the pieces of the previous day. I have a big couch because I'm a big guy, and it's not unheard of for me to fall asleep on it watching TV or reading. It's less common not to remember a lot of what happened before that. I moved forward in time, from my first visit to Mary Miller, to the trip to Carfagna's, to the younger version of Sophia Loren, to the second trip to Mary's house and my encounter with Freddie and Darryl, and then on to the game, which I dimly recalled Ohio State had won, convincingly. I recalled a couple of boxes of pizza and several cans of Black Label. And then nothing. Slowly, with a groan, I rolled onto my side. Hopalong stared up at me accusingly.

"You again," I said.

It took a long time to get moving. After shaving and some coffee, I limped around Schiller Park with the dog once without collapsing. It wasn't until I got back that it dawned on me my busted doorjamb had been fixed, including a shiny new lock. Roy. He must have done it after I'd passed out on the couch.

I followed my Sunday routine in slow motion, including the embarrassing concession of driving to Cup o' Joe instead of walking. I was settled into my usual chair by 10 a.m., and by

10:45 I was buzzing on two cups of coffee as I read the *Dispatch's* wall-to-wall coverage of the game. The number one question now consuming Columbus, as it did every year, was whether the Buckeyes could pull it off next week against Michigan.

I was pulling into my customary space by the judge's townhouse when my cell phone went off. I looked at my watch. I had five minutes to spare.

"It's Mary Miller."

"Morning," I said.

A pause. "Are you all right?"

"I'm not going to the gym today, if that's what you mean. But I'll live. How about you?"

As though she hadn't heard me, she said, "You wanted to know where Danny worked."

"That's right."

"After you left, I was digging around in the back room a little."

"Where the baby sleeps."

Another pause. "Right. Whatever. Anyway, I found a piece of paper from the place. Some kind of form he was carrying around. It's got the name of the company on it."

"Great," I said.

"The thing is . . ."

I waited.

"Thing is, I wondered if it might be worth something to you."

"Worth it how?"

"Worth, like, helping me out."

"You mean, beyond saving you from Freddie and Darryl?"

"Even Steven," she said, tossing my phrase back at me.

"OK," I said. "Help how?"

"Like I said, Danny screwed me on the rent."

"I give you some money for rent, you tell me where he worked."

"Something like that."

"How about, exactly like that?"

"Sure," she said. "That's what I meant."

"Tell you what," I said. "Little bit of money up front for the info. If it pans out, I give you the rest right afterward."

"How much?"

"Give you a hundred bucks."

"Today?"

"Your landlord works on Sunday?"

She paused. "I'm out of groceries too," she said.

I looked at my watch. I was now one minute late.

"All right," I said. "Give me a couple hours. I'll be by."

NOT THAT MANY MINUTES later, lying beside the judge, that is to say, Laura, neither of us clothed, I reached out and took her hand. She let me hold it for all of two seconds before pulling it away.

After a few more moments, I said, "I was thinking."

"Oh?"

"You know where Bethel Road is?"

"Of course."

"You know how it's this mecca of Indian and East Asian restaurants."

"I'll take your word for it."

"So there's a new Thai place up there, just opened."

"OK."

"Got a good review in the paper."

"Fascinating."

"I was thinking of trying it out. Maybe for dinner."

"Admirable of you."

"And I was wondering if you wanted to join me."

Silence.

After a minute, she said, "Join you for dinner?"

"That's right."

We were both lying on our backs, staring at the ceiling. She had been unusually solicitous when I'd come into her office and she'd seen how slowly I was moving. Not enough to ask for the details, but something like pity had crossed her face. She had even helped pull my shirt off when we migrated to her bedroom. A first. I didn't let little details like the fact I'd been incapable of doing it myself ruin the beauty of the moment.

She said, "I don't think so."

More silence. More lying on our backs.

"Maybe another time," I said.

"Andy."

"Yes?"

"That's not part of the deal."

"The deal."

"With you."

"With us."

Still staring at the ceiling, she said, "I'm not comfortable with expanding our relationship. I'm sorry. What we have right now works for me."

I thought back to when we met. One of Burke's Christmas parties. Casual pleasantries exchanged. My usual chauvinistic comment to myself: *pretty good-looking for a judge.* Then the call, out of the blue, a couple of weeks later. She needed an escort home for a few days while police looked into some threats she'd received from the brother of a lowlife she'd sent to prison. Something between a driver and a bodyguard. Off the record and off the books. The judge divorced. Two kids, both in college. Sometime between the third and fourth week, around the time the threat risk was arrested, the arrangement morphed from business into whatever we had now. Business casual?

The odd thing was, we'd almost never discussed the transition. It just sort of happened.

I said, "Sorry I brought it up."

After a moment, she said, "It's all right. Just don't let it happen again."

With more effort than I cared to admit to, I propped myself up on an elbow and looked at her. She was smiling.

"Kidding," she said.

"Right," I replied.

# 22

THE WOMAN WHO ANSWERED THE PHONE
at J&B Construction Monday morning either didn't know
who Reilly was or was a sweet-sounding liar, but either way
couldn't tell me anything about him. With a little wheedling I
was able to pry from her the name of the person who might
be able to, a company principal named Tommy Watkins, and
with a little more wheedling I persuaded her to tell me where
I could find him. Even my charm couldn't separate his cell
phone number from her, though, and so I got in my van and
drove over to the New Albany construction site where she
promised he'd be available.

I found the project easily, noting as I pulled into a gravel
parking lot that I was less than a mile from the Freeleys' house.
As I walked up to the double-wide trailer serving as the project
office, I thought about my brief meeting with Mary Miller the
afternoon before, after I'd driven from the judge's to her apartment with the money. She'd handed me a piece of paper.

"I can write the information down," I said. "If you want to
keep it."

"I don't want it," she replied. "Got no need for anything of his."

A burly guy wearing a J&B Construction hardhat answered the trailer door. After I explained what I needed, he got on a radio, and after a couple of minutes an even burlier guy walked up to where I was standing.

"Tommy Watkins?" I said.

"Who are you?"

I told him, handed him my card. He stared at it, then handed it back.

"What do you want."

"I need some information about Danny Reilly."

"What about him?"

"I'm trying to find out where he was the last few days."

"You know he's dead, right?"

"I know."

"So what does it matter."

"It matters to me. Was he working here? This site?"

"Can't say."

"Why not?"

"Because I don't want to. Because I don't have to. Because you need to get off my job site right now."

Tommy Watkins was a big guy, as big as me, and even if his stomach suggested he'd enjoyed a few too many beers over the years, he looked like most of him was still muscle.

"I'm just trying to get a little information about him. That's all."

"For what."

"For a case."

"What kind of case."

"Can't really get into it."

"Then get lost."

"Just a couple quick questions?"

Watkins took a step closer toward me and without saying a word jerked his head in the direction of my van. I couldn't think of anything snappy to say, and even if I'd thought about getting physical, I was at the moment just lucky to be vertical. No other choice: I just walked away.

"HELLO," MARY MILLER SAID a few minutes later. I'd pulled into the parking lot of New Albany High School to collect my thoughts.

"Your information was good," I said. "About J&B."

"Good for you. That mean I'm getting the rest of my money?"

"All in good time," I said. "Name Tommy Watkins mean anything to you?"

"No. Should it?"

"Construction manager. Big guy. Not happy."

"Tommy?"

"That's right."

"Sounds like his boss."

"That's the one."

"What about him?"

"How'd you know he was Danny's boss?"

"Heard him complain about him a couple times."

"About what?"

"About nothing."

"He just threw me off a building site. All it took was a mention of Danny's name."

"I don't think they got along."

"Any idea why not?"

"Listen," she said. "What about the rest of my money?"

"You'll get it," I said. "I just need a little more information first."

"Why should I tell you anything?"

"Because I'm trying to help you here. I can see what kind of guy Danny was. What he did to you."

"So what. He's dead now."

"And another thing," I said. "The 'Night Shift'?"

"What about it?"

"I don't care if Danny's dead or on the moon. That stuff is still hanging over him. Police find out about that, they'll be back to visit. And this time they will have a search warrant. Whether your baby's sleeping or not."

"I didn't have anything to do with that," she protested.

"They might see it differently, seeing as it's in your apartment."

"So you're going to be the rat who sics the cops on me."

"Wrong," I said. "I'm going to be your friend when someone else rats on you. Big difference."

Silence. I could hear the TV on loud in the background. *Price Is Right,* if I wasn't mistaken.

"Well?" I said.

She said, "Danny had a thing going with painkillers."

"Taking them?"

"Selling them. Popular on construction sites. Lot of these guys get injured, they go to a doctor and they walk out with two bottles of Oxy. Two weeks later they're addicted."

"OK."

"That guy Tommy was buying from Danny."

"You sure?"

"I'm sure."

"So he told me to take a hike because he thought I'd found out."

"Not quite," she said.

IT WAS ALMOST TEN o'clock when I hung up with Mary. I still had to pay Bobby Fletcher a visit, and I had my thrice-weekly appointment with Honey Huntington to consider, noon sharp. But I knew I had no choice but to turn around.

"I thought I told you to get lost," Watkins said, his face darkening when he saw me approach.

"Short-term memory loss," I said. "So listen carefully, because I don't want to have to repeat myself. Reilly was dealing painkillers, and you were a customer. Know how many people would be interested in knowing that? Starting with the doctors whose pretty new office you're building. How do you think they're going to feel if the place isn't plumb because you were high while it went up?"

Watkins's face was stone. Impossible to read. "Who told you that?" he said.

"It doesn't matter. And I don't really care one way or the other myself. But you're going to care if I don't get a couple questions answered."

He looked around. A couple other guys had arrived by now, and one of them was looking at us in a questioning fashion. Watkins waved him off.

"It's not me," he said, lowering his voice.

"What's not you?"

"The pills. They're not for me. They're for my wife."

"Your wife?"

"She fell down the stairs, about six months ago. Carrying laundry. Slipped on something. Wrenched the hell out of her back."

"Sorry to hear that."

"She couldn't walk for a couple of days. Doctor gave her a prescription for hydrocodone. I didn't think anything about it, especially because it seemed to help. Then all of a sudden I realized something was wrong. She was acting funny. Find out she's addicted."

"It happens."

"Her prescriptions ran out, and the doctor wouldn't fill them again. She was getting desperate. I wasn't sure what to do."

"Reilly found out."

He nodded. "I knew it wasn't right. But I had to do something. She was going crazy. I kept saying each time would be the last."

"Counseling?"

"Sure," he said. "I've got twenty thousand dollars just lying around for a thirty-day stay. Gimme a break."

"So each time was going to be the last. Except the last time really was. Danny stiffed you, didn't he?"

"How do you know that?"

"Just answer the question."

"He told me his supply had run short. That it would only be a couple of days. But I'd given him two hundred dollars in advance. Like an idiot. And I was desperate. Tina was down to a handful. Reilly just laughed at me. Patted me on the cheek. Told me to relax. He'd take care of everything."

"That must have made you mad."

"Of course it did."

"Mad enough to do something about it."

"I was desperate."

"Mad enough to kill him? Confront him, shoot him, and get your money back?"

Watkins's eyes widened, in shock. "No," he said. "Nothing like that. Don't be crazy."

"I'm not crazy. I'm just doing the math. And the numbers say you had a really good reason to want Reilly dead."

"I didn't kill Reilly," he said, recovering a bit. His voice got a bit gruffer, and some of the steel I'd sensed earlier in the day returned. "Believe me, I wanted to. And I could have. But I didn't."

"What are you going to do," I said. "About your wife."

He looked at me, angrily. "That's none of your business."

I stepped a bit closer to him. "It's all my business, now that everything's on the table. Which brings up the only thing I really wanted to know: Where was Reilly working?"

"I don't have to tell you that."

"True," I said. "So maybe I'll ask the suits downtown at J&B at the same time I'm letting them know their foreman was involved in drug deals on the job site."

This time, Watkins looked like it was me he wanted to kill. But after a moment, he said, "We've got a home construction line. Few new builds, McMansions, but mainly high-end renovations. Danny was working on one of those the past few weeks."

"Where?"

"Around the corner."

"Address."

He told me. I scribbled it in my notebook.

"Anything else?" Watkins said, staring at me. "I've got work to do."

"Yes, there is," I said. "Reilly was on your payroll when he died. For obvious reasons he never picked up his last check. I need it."

"You've got to be kidding."

I shook my head. "You're not the only one Reilly owed money to."

"He owed you? Is that what this is all about?"

"You think I'd ever get short with a guy like Reilly? Somebody else who knew him. That I'm helping."

"There is no check," Watkins said.

"Why not."

"That's not how Reilly got paid."

"Under the table? That's perfect."

"I'm not saying anything more about it. That's just the way it was."

"So what do I do to get his money?"

"You don't do anything. There is no money."

"Wanna bet?"

An hour later, I was at J&B's small headquarters downtown on North Fifth Street in an up-and-coming warehouse district. When I walked in, a young woman at a receptionist's desk handed me an envelope without even saying hello.

"Thank you," I said.

"Have a nice day," she replied, in a voice that implied the opposite. I didn't blame her. My stomach was hurting. Watkins was a broken man, and I'd broken him even further. I'd threatened to reveal his secret to his bosses to find out where Reilly had been working, and I'd threatened him again to finagle a whopping $300 out of the downtown petty cash fund. He'd stepped away from me when he made the call downtown, and I didn't hear everything that was said. But I had a strong feeling that the money would come out of his pay one way or the other. That made me feel even worse. Reilly had cheated a sick woman out of the pills she needed and stolen money from her husband. I no doubt had only made it worse. But a central question remained: could Watkins have been angry enough at Reilly to kill him? He'd denied it adamantly, but who wouldn't?

I sighed. The list of people who wanted Reilly dead just kept getting longer. Only question was, who crossed the line into action?

I HAD JUST ENOUGH time to formulate a mental list of the suspects and check it twice—I was stuck on naughty, since nobody seemed nice—before I arrived in Bexley, mindful of Henry Huntington's admonition that I cover that noon to 2 p.m. slot like a hawk. He'd reminded me of it just the day before, checking in again by phone to see how it was going. Today, Honey rewarded me with a break in her routine, driving not to the Short North for another round of afternoon delight but out east, way out east, to a nondescript office building in Reynoldsburg, a suburb a few miles farther out from Bexley and a few notches further down on the per capita income rankings. After Honey had gone inside, I waited ten minutes, put on my sunglasses and Clippers cap, then followed in her tracks. I walked past some ferns and a framed picture of Ohio Stadium on game day, went to the elevators, and nonchalantly perused the list of tenants between the two doors. The menu was eclectic: law firm, some accountants, a dental practice, a financial planning office, an insurance company, and, hello, Farnsworth and Farnsworth, certified marriage counselors. Discreetly, I pulled out my phone and took a picture of the tenant list, then a second one zooming in on the Farnsworths. I thought about this latest twist. Despite the obvious signs that Honey wasn't happy at home, there was still something nagging at me about this case, something I couldn't put my finger on. But either way, I thought, as followed Honey back to Bexley, things weren't looking good for the Huntingtons' future happiness.

# 23

FLOWER HAVEN NURSING HOME OFF KARL
Road on the north side was an undistinguished facility with
one big exception: the full-size scarlet-and-gray RV sitting in
the parking lot. The Band Wagon's custom paint job featured
an enormous Ohio State logo and, from one side to the other,
airbrushed portraits of the program's six Heisman trophy winners, including my dog's namesake, Howard "Hopalong" Cas-
sady, smack in the middle. The satellite dish on top would have
been the envy of more than one local TV affiliate. Even the
tires were school colors. I knew well, too well, of Fletcher's
love of the Buckeyes, but this was the most blatant tribute I
had come across yet.

Walking into the lobby, I was greeted by an enormous
Ohio State banner hanging across the rear wall. A glass case
held several shelves of helmets, jerseys, and game balls. Scarlet-
and-gray afghans were folded neatly over the top of the room's
armchairs and couches. A framed oil painting of Woody Hayes
hung over a fireplace. The pillows on the couches were Ohio
State–themed, as were the coasters on the coffee and lamp

tables, the lampshades themselves, and, I saw as I approached the woman sitting at a registration desk, her earrings, the sweater she was wearing, and the coffee cup beside her computer mouse. Which was also scarlet and gray.

"Yes?" she said sweetly, which in those surroundings could only mean she didn't recognize me.

"I was wondering if Mr. Fletcher was available," I said, and handed her my card.

"I know he's had some appointments, but let me just see."

She picked up the phone and dialed an extension and after a moment informed Fletcher he had a visitor. It was almost amusing—almost—to watch the change that came over her face after she gave him my name and heard his reaction.

"He's in the Band Wagon," she said curtly, when she'd hung up.

As I strode across the lobby, I could hear her typing furiously, and I knew the odds were just about even it was my name being Googled. I'd seen it happen before.

Walking back out, I stopped and held the door to let a woman come inside. She was pretty, and I snuck a second glance. About my age, maybe a bit younger. Athlete's figure. Nice-fitting jeans, a patterned green blouse, and a trim dark jacket. A mound of bright red hair wrestled into submission by a green hair band that matched her eyes, and all of that punctuated, as it were, by a striking scar running down the left side of her face.

As she passed she glanced at me, and a startled expression crossed her face. Had seen that happen before too. She looked for just a moment as if she were going to say something, then appeared to reconsider. "Excuse me," she said, her eyes dropping, as she stepped to the side and went into the lobby.

Outside, there was no need to knock on the Band Wagon door. Fletcher was standing at the entrance, waiting. He had to be in his midsixties by now, balding, a little bigger around the middle than I remembered but still pretty trim. He wore gray

trousers, a white button-down shirt, and a red—sorry, scarlet—
sweater vest.

"Andy," he said. "Good to see you."

"Go to hell," I said.

INSIDE THE RV, THE 1969 Rose Bowl was playing on
a TV opposite the couch I sank into. In the kitchen, a rack of
Ohio State–branded grilling utensils hung from a scarlet-and-
gray cabinet. Down the hall, toward the rear, I spied a half-
sized Buckeyes pool table.

"I'll give you this," Fletcher said. "It took a lot of balls for
you to come here."

"Don't flatter yourself," I said.

"I'm just saying—"

"You're not saying anything," I said. "You're listening."

I said, keeping my eye on the TV, "A few nights ago, Freddie Carmichael and Darryl Nysong broke into my house and
tossed the place. They were looking for a laptop that someone
had given me."

I looked at Fletcher. He looked at me, then the game.

"Unfortunately for them, it wasn't in the house at the time."

"I have no idea what you're talking about," Fletcher said.

I ignored him. "A couple of hours after they broke in, a
guy named Danny Reilly paid me a visit in the alley around the
corner from my house. This time I had the laptop, and when I
came to it was missing."

"Still no clue."

I kept going, explaining about Reilly and Grandview Yard
quarry and Mary Miller—though I kept her name and where
she lived out of it, not that it mattered—and on to my run-
in with Darryl and Freddie at Mary's apartment. When I was
finished, I leaned back and looked around. I had to admit, the
setup was nice. This might have been Fletcher's best ever.

"So what?" Fletcher said.

"Freddie and Darryl and I had a little conversation when it was all over. They explained nicely that you sent them to look for the laptop."

"Hell they did."

"So my question is, why's a prick like you so interested in a laptop that you'd send hired help around to beat people up for it. Or maybe even kill."

"Kill? What are you talking about?"

"Danny Reilly didn't put that bullet in himself," I said. "You give the order or did they just freelance on him? Either way, you're responsible."

"Jesus Christ," Fletcher said. "You think I killed this Reilly guy? Is that what you're saying?"

"That's what I'm saying."

"You're crazy. You're fucking crazy. I didn't have anything to do with that."

"Reilly wanted the laptop. You want the laptop. Why?"

"Get the hell out of here, Hayes," he said.

"Call me Andy."

"Call you fucking nothing," he said. "I said, get out."

"Or what? You'll call Freddie and Darryl for round two? Did you ask them how it went with Reilly's girlfriend, by the way?"

"Get out!"

"You know, you might want to consider why they keep coming up short. Have you noticed you keep sending them after the laptop and they keep fucking up? Is it possible that Coach Fletcher is getting screwed by his B squad?"

"You're insane, do you know that? You, of all people, coming here. Making these kinds of allegations."

"You still haven't answered my question."

"Which is?"

"What's the big deal with this laptop?"

Fletcher had turned red by now, and for a moment I thought he might be having some kind of attack. His forehead was shiny, and he swallowed a few times. He pulled himself together enough to say, "Get the hell out of here or I'm going to have you arrested."

I laughed. "Arrested? Listen to yourself." I looked at him, hard. "Do you hear what I'm saying? *Listen to yourself.* You'll have me arrested?"

"OK, calm down. I didn't mean it that way."

"Of course you didn't."

"I just got a little upset."

"Perfectly understandable."

"But I still don't know what you're talking about."

"You were always a bad liar, Bobby," I said. "Unlike me."

His breathing had evened out now, and a hard look, a look I remembered well, came over his face.

"A lot of time has passed," he said.

"That it has."

"The jury's still on my side. You're the one who tore the heart out of every fan in this city. In this state. Not me. Nobody knows who I am. But everybody knows who you are."

"Thanks to you."

"No," he said. "Thanks to you. And don't ever forget that. Thanks to you."

I thought of a million other things I could say, but in the end kept my mouth shut. This wasn't getting me anywhere closer to the laptop, and it was taking me someplace else I wasn't ready to go.

"I'm leaving," I said, standing up. "But I'm going to be back. And I'm going to find out why you want that laptop. And if you had anything to do with Reilly, I'm going to find that out too. And I don't care if every person in this city hates me. At least I know where I stand. At least my sins are right where people can see them."

I went to walk out the door, but Fletcher moved in front of me.

"You know why people hate you, Hayes? Because you fucked Ohio State over for money. Judas's silver. And that's what you are. Nothing but a fucking *Judas*. That's what everyone in town thinks of you. That's why you're not going to win this one. Nobody will ever hate me as much as they hate you."

I leaned in toward him. I didn't mind being called a Judas, because I had been called far worse back in the day. And probably deservedly so.

"I made a mistake," I said, pushing my face close to his. "A big one, thanks to you. But it was my own mistake. I didn't send a couple of no-neck nothings to run my errands and then lie about it. I had the guts to fuck things up all by myself." I leaned closer still. "And I didn't kill anyone." I stared hard, and realized I could see the tiny capillaries in his eyes, which looked bloodshot and tired.

"Not yet, anyway," I added.

I didn't give him a chance to respond. I walked out of the Band Wagon without shutting the door.

That would show him.

I HAD CROSSED THE parking lot and had the door to my van open when I heard her voice.

"Excuse me?"

I looked around. The redhead I'd held the door for was walking quickly toward me. I waited, against my better judgment.

"You're Andy Hayes, aren't you?" she said.

"That's right."

"I was wondering if we could talk."

"Talk?"

"That's right. But not here."

"Any particular topic?"

She paused. Glanced in the direction of the Band Wagon. Glanced back.

"About the laptop," she said. "It's all my fault."

# 24

I BROUGHT TWO BLACK COFFEES TO OUR
table at the Wendy's up the street. It's a fast food chain, but it's
headquartered in suburban Columbus, so it fits my definition
of local business.

"Thanks," she said.

"You're welcome." I glanced discreetly at her scar, then
looked away.

"Thanks for meeting with me."

"Welcome," I said again.

She took a sip of coffee. She said, "My name's Anne Cooper,
by the way."

"Nice to meet you, Anne Cooper."

"I know Doug Freeley."

"Well, well," I said.

Another sip. "This is difficult."

"Take your time."

She looked away, toward the restaurant door, then back again.

"Like I said, this is all my fault."

"How?"

"This whole thing. With the laptop. I never meant for any of this to happen. And now I'm in trouble. Big trouble. And I don't know what to do."

"Why don't you back up. Start at the beginning."

She said, "Bobby can't know I'm here. It was a gamble just talking to you in the parking lot."

"You know Fletcher?"

"Know him? I work for him."

SHE SIGHED. CLEARED A strand of red hair away from her eyes. They were amazingly green.

"I'm an English teacher," she said. "At Columbus State. I'm adjunct, but I'm hoping to get a full-time job."

"All right," I said.

"A few months ago an e-mail went around asking if anyone was interested in doing some tutoring. Nothing to do with Columbus State, just a freelance thing. I needed the money, so I decided to check it out."

"With you so far."

"I called the number, and it turns out it was Fletcher. I went to meet him. We sat in the Band Wagon."

"Quaint place."

"It's stunning. I'd never seen anything like it, and I'm from a family of big-time Buckeye fans."

"He was the one looking for a tutor?"

"He had some young persons that needed help with their writing. That's how he put it. 'Young persons.' Taking some college classes and struggling a bit. Needed a helping hand. He kept using that phrase. 'Just a helping hand.'"

"OK," I said.

"He offered me two hundred dollars per tutoring session, twice a week. I couldn't turn it down. I have a lot of debts at the moment. That was my car payment plus groceries."

"I'm listening."

"Anyway, I met with the 'young persons' the next day. Of course I figured it out immediately. I don't know why Fletcher felt he had to disguise the whole thing. I even recognized one of their names. All three were football players. Not any of the stars, but linchpins, if you know what I mean."

"I know what you mean."

She blushed. "Duh," she said. "Sorry."

"Don't worry about it. I'm honored you forgot who I was for five minutes."

She looked at me to see if I were teasing her. I smiled as best I could and encouraged her to continue.

"It didn't take me long to realize I was more than a tutor. They were all in some kind of remedial writing class that required a lot of short papers, three to five pages, that kind of thing. The idea was I write the papers for them. They briefed me on the class, what they thought the teacher had been saying, and I took notes. I'd write up the papers, trying not to make them too smarty-pants sounding, and deliver them the next lesson."

"University know about this? Athletic department?"

"Not at all. It was all Fletcher. All his deal."

"Where was he during all this?"

"Floating on the edges, at first."

"At first?"

"There's these two guys that work for Fletcher. Ex-players. Maintenance crew sorts. Kind of."

"Freddie and Darryl."

"You know them?"

"We've met," I said. "They broke into my house last week, although I wasn't there at the time. We had a more intimate encounter Saturday."

"Oh my God," she said. "Don't tell me—"

"The laptop," I said. "It's OK. It's the most popular piece of equipment I've ever possessed. I'm just trying to figure out why."

She looked down for a moment.

"It's OK," I said.

"No, it's not."

"Please."

After a minute, she said, "Fletcher was around at first. But later it was Freddie and Darryl coming in. To check on us. They never said or did anything. But the message was loud and clear. This was Bobby's little secret, and they were going to make sure it stayed that way."

"Or else?"

She nodded. "Maybe not physical harm. But if word ever got out about what I'd done, I'd be ruined. Fired. And bankrupt: I've got creditors lined up a mile behind me. And it's not just me. I've got a daughter. I've got to think of her. This job was my chance to fix everything."

"The laptop?" I said.

"It's got all the papers on it," she said. "Everything I wrote. And the names of the kids I've been helping. And e-mails from Fletcher."

"Is it yours?"

"That's right. Thought it made sense for me to use it. It's my work, after all. I only figured out later it also meant nothing attached Fletcher to the tutoring. Except me."

Something occurred to me.

I said, "You're Acooper."

"Sorry?"

"The user name: 'Acooper.' And the password: 'JarJarBinks-MustDie.' Taped to the underside."

"The underside?"

"That's where it was when I got it. You didn't do that?"

"No," she said. "Unless—"

"Unless what?"

"Maybe Doug did it."

"Why would Doug know your username and password?"

"I told him."

"Why?"

"It's complicated."

"I can tell. You said nothing tied the tutoring to Fletcher. Because it was your laptop."

"Right. But he knows his e-mails are on it. Those get out . . ."

"So Fletcher has a strong motive for you to get it back. Fair enough. But how does Doug fit into all this?"

She reddened again. "That's where it gets complicated."

"I'm still listening."

"I appreciate that."

I waited.

She said, "I met Doug a couple of months ago. At the nursing home. Right after I started."

"Doug Freeley came to Flower Haven?"

She nodded. "Something to do with the business. He was helping with Fletcher's books somehow."

I thought about this for a minute. "Accounts receivable," I said.

"I'm sorry?"

"Freeley's company. American Financial Health Care. They buy up the debt of health care places, like nursing homes, small hospitals."

"Makes more sense now, I guess. Why Doug was here. He was always a little vague about it."

"He's vague with a lot of people. If that's any consolation."

"It's not. But thanks."

"So you met Doug."

"In the lobby one day. Bobby introduced us. We had a nice chat. Doug can be very, you know, charming."

I thought of the cold scene in the Freeleys' living room. Of the hard look on Beth Freeley's face. I nodded.

"We talked about James Thurber. Turns out he's quite a fan."

I nodded again. I too was a fan of the humorist from Columbus. But I was thinking it was one of the few things Freeley and I had in common.

"That's how it started," Anne said, taking another sip of coffee. Her voice sounded distant, almost as if she were talking to herself.

She said, "I was lonely and stressed about money. Unbelievably stressed. That, and other things. And like I said, he was charming. Warm. Understanding. I'm not proud of it, you know. But he was the first man who'd paid attention to me in a while. In a way that I needed."

"You had an affair," I said.

"Having," she said. "At least I think we still are."

"Complicated," I said.

"Right."

I was trying to think what else to say when Anne's purse made a sound like someone was inside, yelling. She dipped into the bag and pulled out her cell phone. "Sorry," she said. "My mom." Her fingers flew over the screen's virtual keys. When she was done she dropped it back into her purse. "It's amazing. She got her first smart phone last year, sixty-five years old, and they had to up the data plan twice."

"Your text alert is a Wookie," I said, placing the sound. "From *Star Wars*. And now your computer password makes a little more sense."

She smiled for the first time that afternoon. "I teach a science fiction class at Columbus State. That's sort of my thing."

"Science fiction class," I said. "Sounds fun."

"It is for me," she said. "Students all sign up for it thinking it's a gut, and then I explain we'll be reading a book a week and writing multiple papers. It drops off after that."

"There goes my plans for auditing it," I said.

She smiled. I smiled. I thought about a parallel universe in which I was auditing a class about science fiction taught by green-eyed Anne Cooper.

"Anyway," she said.

"Right."

"So we went down to Hocking County last week."

"Hocking County?"

"Doug and I. They've got a getaway cabin down there. Doug made up a story about a business trip. For Beth, I mean. Not the smartest idea in hindsight. The guy he was supposed to be on the trip with called the house to see if Doug wanted to golf. This was the next day, Saturday. We were driving into Athens for breakfast when Beth called. Just our luck—cell service is so spotty down there you usually can't get through. She was furious. We had to pack up and leave in a hurry. Somehow in all the excitement I left my laptop in his car."

"When was this?"

"Last Friday and Saturday."

I did the math. The same night as Ted Hamilton's party. Somehow Pete Freeley must have found the laptop and transferred the video.

"That explains things a bit more," I said.

"Sort of," Anne said.

"Sort of?"

"We had a nice night together. On Friday. The cabin has a hot tub. And there's a fireplace."

I nodded, not sure what to say.

"But afterward, you know, I woke up briefly and saw Doug at the counter in the kitchen. It's one of these bar things that jut out, with stools and all that. He had my laptop open. I asked him what he was doing. He said something about borrowing it for work. I was pretty tired and didn't think much of it and went back to sleep. But the next morning I asked him about it again."

"What did he say?"

"He got this funny look on his face. He was nervous and I pushed it a little, and finally he said he'd put some work files on it. He needed someplace secure, just as backup. I asked him what kind of files and he was vague. 'Financial stuff,' that sort of thing. He said it would be all right, almost implied Fletcher had cleared it."

"Had he?"

"I don't know. I still didn't think that much about it. It was only later that I got to wondering."

I thought about this scenario for a moment.

I said, "A minute ago, you said you told Doug the password. Is this the part where it's complicated?"

She blushed a little. "I guess so, yes."

I waited.

"He'd asked me for it, the night before."

"Why?"

"We were going to watch a movie. He said the cabin's DVD player was on the fritz. He saw that I'd brought my laptop and asked if we could use that instead."

"He didn't have his own?"

"He had a tablet. But no movies on it. That's what he said. And you can't stream anything down there."

"The DVD player. Was it really not working?"

"Doug said it wasn't."

"Did you test it?"

She shook her head.

"So it's possible he made it up so he could use your laptop, get the password."

"It's possible," she said, looking miserable.

"Just a theory," I said.

Anne said, "You're probably right. Whatever he put on the laptop must have been really important."

"Why do you say that?"

"Saturday morning, on our way into Athens for breakfast. He was so insistent I bring it. Even though we were planning to come back to the cabin. He said you could never be too careful down there. Break-ins, that kind of thing. But there was the TV, right there, you know? He didn't worry about that."

"Did he say why he put the files on the laptop? As opposed to anyplace else? A thumb drive, for example?"

"He didn't trust them."

"Didn't trust thumb drives?"

"Said he lost files that way once. Misplaced it. Wanted something bigger. 'Bigger than a breadbox,' he said."

"Not that a laptop's that big."

"No," she said. "He was speaking metaphorically, I guess."

Or lying, I thought. Putting the files onto Anne's computer was risky, but it also served the purpose of making them someone else's problem as well. Nice way to treat your mistress, but who's counting? That said, the plan might have worked if Doug's golfing buddy hadn't accidentally busted him with the result that the laptop ended up at his house instead of Anne's. It seemed a little odd that Doug would have left such a precious commodity lying around where Pete was then able to borrow it for his own nefarious purposes. But that detail was no doubt lost in the chaos that Doug confronted when he arrived home and faced the wrath of Beth. I had some familiarity with that type of chaos in my own past.

"Thoughts?" Anne said.

I didn't say anything. I was thinking about the laptop. It had attracted a lot of interesting files in a short period of time: ghost-written English papers; the video of Ted Hamilton and Jennifer Rawlings; some kind of iffy financial data from American Financial Health Care. I thought about the beatings I'd taken for it. There were a lot of people with a strong interest in getting the machine back. Yet none of those things seemed connected. Was it possible I'd suffered a near concussion because of the world's biggest coincidence?

I interrupted my own reverie. "Did you watch any movies?" I said.

"What?"

"The laptop. Did you end up using it to watch movies? Like Doug said."

"We started to. He got out some wine, lit a fire. Very romantic. He knew I was into science fiction and so he'd bought me the whole *Battlestar Galactica* series as a present. It was really nice of him."

"I bet it was. He set the laptop up?"

"We started to watch. But, you know"—she looked down—"we didn't get far."

I looked away. "Right."

"And then I fell asleep. And when I woke up he was working on it."

"He told you it was missing? Later?"

She nodded. "I realized what happened when we got back. I'd left it in his car. I texted him and he told me it was gone. Mentioned your visit. Then I told Bobby."

"What'd Bobby say?

"Said if I didn't get it back this week he's going to fire me. And if that happens, I don't know what I'll do. That tutoring was the only thing keeping me afloat."

"Not that it matters," I said. "But did you tell Bobby about me?"

Now she looked more miserable. And her eyes began to shine.

"I did," she said. "After Doug texted me and told me what was happening. After you went to their house. I'm sorry. I'm so sorry."

"Don't worry about it," I said. "At least that explains how Freddie and Darryl knew where to look."

"The stupid thing is, I actually thought it would help my cause."

"What do you mean?"

"You know. 'It's OK. There's a *private eye* on the case.' Thought that would ease Fletcher's mind. How stupid could I be."

"It's all right," I said. "You couldn't have known."

"I'm sorry," she said again.

I thought about what Anne had told me. I thought about the things I knew about Fletcher I couldn't tell her. I thought about some other stuff. Finally, because it was all I could think to do, I leaned back and said, "'So you're the little woman who wrote the book that made this great war.'"

Anne looked at me, puzzled. Then the lightbulb went off. "Abraham Lincoln to Harriet Beecher Stowe," she said. "How odd that you would say something like that to me."

"Because a dumb jock isn't supposed to know that quote?"

"Because you're making light of a serious problem."

"Well," I said, thinking about it. No one had ever put it quite like that before.

I said, "I guess that's what I do. I make light of serious problems." I leaned forward and looked at her, straight into her amazing green eyes. "And then I fix them."

# 25

BUSINESS WAS STARTING TO PICK UP AT THE Wendy's. Several teenagers crowded the counter. I looked at my watch. Four-thirty.

"Do you need to go?" Anne said.

"Not really."

"Do you mind if I tell you something?"

"I guess not."

"You're nothing like what I expected."

"Thank you," I said. "I think."

"Like I said, I grew up in a big Buckeyes family. I mean, who doesn't around here. But my dad and my uncles and my brothers are huge fans. And they, you know, idolized you."

"They shouldn't have."

"Maybe not. But they did."

"You?"

"I was definitely into it. It was fun, the games and the parties. It's just in your blood, in Columbus."

"And then."

"When it happened, people couldn't believe it. I'm not sure my dad has forgiven you even now."

"You're kidding. Even after all the heart-to-hearts we've had?"

She laughed. "I know it sounds silly. But it's like they thought they knew you. Like you were their friend."

"Sure," I said. "I get that a lot."

"And then . . ."

"I betrayed them."

"No!" she said. "I mean, yes. I mean—that's how they saw it."

"How everybody did."

"Ridiculous."

"Not really."

"I mean, afterward. My brother went around for a week. 'Hayes,' he kept saying. 'Benedict Fucking Hayes. They ought to hang him too.'"

"He had a point."

"Worst thing?"

"Yes?"

"I was the same way."

"You weren't alone."

"When Doug told me you were involved. I couldn't believe it."

"Most people can't."

"Like I said, you're not what I expected."

"Which was?"

"I don't know," she said. "More—" She paused.

"More Captain Kirk, less Captain Picard?"

"Exactly," she said, brightening. "That's exactly it."

"On the other hand."

"Yes?"

"What your brother said about Benedict Arnold?"

"Oh?"

"Maybe he wasn't that far off. Other than the fact that people forget Benedict Arnold died peacefully in England after several successes as a British Army officer."

"So?"

I shrugged. "So maybe that just makes me a successful traitor."

I GOT US MORE coffee and we kept talking. I wheedled out of her that she was from Grove City, a suburb on the south-west side. Went to Denison University in Granville, just east of Columbus. Alma mater of Woody Hayes, I reminded her. She laughed. Earned a Ph.D. at Indiana University in Bloomington. Met her husband there. *Late husband,* she added quietly. Taught at a small state school in the Finger Lakes in New York State for a while. Daughter was seven. Nothing about the scar—not that I asked.

Just when I was starting to get hungry and wondering how prudent it would be to invite her to dinner, her purse made the *Star Wars* sound again.

She pulled out the phone, looked at it and frowned. Her fingers flew.

"Doug," she said, avoiding my gaze. "Wondering what's up."

"What'd you tell him?"

"I told him I might have a lead on it."

The phone went off again. She looked at the message, bit her lower lip, replied, then tossed the phone back into her purse.

"Sorry," she said. "I text too much."

"Text too much with Doug?"

"Text too much in general."

"The modern malaise."

Her phone went off again. She glanced at her purse, hesitated, then looked back at me.

"Anyway," she said. "What about it?"

"What about what?"

"This," she said, and spread open her hands. "This mess. My mess. Can you really fix it?"

"I don't know," I said. "I'm going to try."

"Is there anything I can do?"

I thought about this. "Keep making yourself useful to Fletcher, I guess. For a little longer."

"What do you mean?"

"He's a loyal person, but only up to a certain point. And only if it involves Ohio State. As long as you can exploit that, we've got time."

"Not sure I understand."

"Right now he's wrestling between firing you because the laptop is gone and trying to figure out how he can keep helping his beloved Buckeyes."

"How do you know that? I mean, that he's thinking all this?"

"I just do," I said.

"Have you met him before?"

"Let's just say we have a history together."

"What kind of history?"

"Just . . ." I said. "Just a history."

"That's it? That's all you can say? After everything I've told you?"

I looked at her. Thought about how much I'd enjoyed meeting her, even under the circumstances. Glanced again at the scar.

"That's it," I said. "For now."

As if reading my mind, or at least watching the movement of my eyes, she nodded slowly.

"One thing at a time," she said.

"Something like that."

We parted ways, Anne explaining she needed to get back to her daughter. I didn't mention dinner after all.

As I drove down 71 it was getting dark and I was starting to ache again. I knew I had more to do, a lot more, starting with Reilly's stepmother, but it would have to wait. I thought of all the food I had at home, the sausage and sauce I'd picked up from Carfagna's. Then I thought about how tired I was. A few minutes later, I was once again at Happy Dragon, picking up more takeout. And a few minutes more after getting home, taking Hopalong around the park, eating my dinner and drinking two cans of Black Label, I was asleep again on the couch.

I think I made it to eight o'clock.

# 26

I WOKE UP THE NEXT MORNING IN A PANIC, sure that I'd forgotten something, missed an appointment, was supposed to be someplace. I checked my phone, but there were no calendar reminders or missed calls. I did, however, have a text from Anne, sent about ten o'clock the night before.

"Doug keeps texting. Says he's desperate. Despondent."

I thought about what I could text back to her but in the end decided to do nothing. The fact that Doug Freeley was despondent was not surprising, given what an apparent mess he'd made of things. The question, like everything else about this case, was: how did it affect me?

A couple hours later I found myself driving up the hill on West Broad Street toward the neighborhood called, appropriately, the Hilltop. I passed the massive state Department of Transportation and Public Safety buildings on the right and, a little farther on, the vacant lot where a building had once stood—before a gas line explosion leveled it—with the welcoming sign "We Buy Used Porn." I passed Lev's Pawn Shop, then Schroeck's Auto Service and Hillcrest Baptist Church and then made my turn. The Hilltop had seen its best days a generation or more ago, though there were high hopes for the new casino that had opened on the site of a defunct Delphi plant a couple of miles down the road. So far the economic development hadn't trickled this far down Broad Street.

I parked my van in front of a worn-down two-story brick house. I opened the gate to the chain-metal fence around the yard, a crowded mess of plastic children's toy slides and play ovens and tricycles, the grass patchy and weedy, and walked up the steps to knock on the door. Ohio State bunting lined the porch railing.

After my second knock a woman wearing jeans and a baggy beige blouse answered the door.

"Brenda Brown?" I said, uncertainly.

"Who are you?"

"Friend of Mary Miller."

"So?" Her hair was pulled back tightly, revealing a wide forehead and a flat, hard-looking face.

"So Mary said you might have something of hers. Something I'm looking for."

Inside the house a child started to wail. "Hang on," the woman said and disappeared. I heard a loud TV, then heard it get louder. The woman was back a moment later.

"Who'd you say you were again?"

"I'm Andy Hayes," I said. "I'm trying to find out who killed Danny Reilly."

WE SAT ON A couch whose springs felt as if they'd given up the ghost around the middle of Bill Clinton's first term. A toddler sat between us watching cartoons on TV while she rubbed cereal into her shirt and hair and occasionally her mouth.

"Granddaughter," Brenda Brown told me. "Jayme."

"Mom at work?"

"Dead," she said. "Overdosed."

"Sorry to hear that."

"Me too. Mary said you might come by."

"She tell you what I was looking for."

"Maybe."

"A laptop. Something Danny took from me."

"Stole?"

"I just need it back," I said.

"What if I don't have it?"

"Mary said your son might have some use for it."

"Maybe," she said. "Why should I tell you?"

"If I get it back, maybe I can find out who killed Danny."

She thought about this. "He didn't deserve to get shot," Brenda said. "I don't care what anybody says."

I said, "What do they say?"

She didn't answer. Glanced at her granddaughter.

I said, "Mary said Danny was from southern Ohio. You happen to know where?"

"Scioto County," Brenda said, pronouncing it Sigh-oh-tah in proper Ohio fashion. "Portsmouth, I think."

"Any idea how long he's been up here?"

"Danny? Not a clue."

"Any guesses?"

"Not really."

"Were you close?" I said.

Brenda laughed. She reached over to a lamp stand beside the couch, picked up a pack of cigarettes, lit one.

She said, "I married his father six years ago. No, seven, and Danny wasn't up here then. We'd see him occasionally. But far as I know he lived in Portsmouth. Didn't even realize he'd moved here."

"Any idea what he did?"

"Did?"

"For work. In Portsmouth."

"Danny? He didn't do a whole hell of a lot of anything, I can tell you that. Not recently, anyway. Not since he'd been out."

"Out?"

She stared at me. "Out of prison."

"Right," I said. Guess that little detail must have slipped Mary Miller's mind. "How long ago was that?"

"Not really sure," Brenda said. Took a drag on the cigarette. "He was in when I met Tom, out when Tom died. I lose track of time in between."

"Tom?"

"Danny's father. Passed two years ago. Lung cancer."

"I'm sorry."

"Me too," she said for the second time that morning. "He and Danny were night and day. Though I think Tom had had his moments, before he became a Christian."

I nodded. "What was Danny in for?"

She shrugged. "Drugs, burglary, theft. I'm not real sure on the details. Tom didn't talk about it and I didn't ask."

"Any idea why Danny stayed down there? After prison?"

"Stayed in Portsmouth? Good question. I know he had a good job at one time. Long time ago. Least that's what Tom said."

"Did he say what kind of job?"

She laughed. "He was a guard. Prison guard."

"Danny was a prison guard?"

"Kind of ironic, isn't it?"

"Do you know where?"

She shook her head. "It wasn't a real prison. I mean, not for adults. Kids. Juvenile center down there someplace."

"Any idea when?"

"Not really. Long time ago, though. Fifteen, twenty years, maybe."

"You know the name of the place?"

"All I know is he had this job, and it was a pretty good job for down there, and then he lost it somehow. That's what Tom said, and that's about all he said. Probably not hard to guess what happened. Drugs or something. Which was kind of par for the course with Danny. Could never quite get anything right. Played some football in high school, according to what Tom told me. Pretty good for not a huge guy. Couple of colleges sniffed around. But he got drunk too many times after games, got into too many fights, got thrown off the team. Close, but no cigar. That was pretty much his whole life. I mean, until he went to prison. You understand what I'm saying?"

I nodded. I had some experience in the realm of missed sports opportunities.

"Why do you care what happened to Danny, anyway?" Brenda said.

Carefully, I said, "If I find out who shot him, I might find out who was trying to get this laptop. And why. But it's kind of a chicken-egg thing. Until I get the laptop back, I can't make a lot of progress with Danny."

Brenda took another pull on her cigarette but didn't say anything.

I said, "No idea why he might have wanted the laptop?"

"Shit, no," Brenda said. "I barely talked to him. I knew Mary, and she was nice. But that's it."

"Any idea where it is?"

"Mary was right—I gave it to my son," Brenda said. "He's into computers. He thought he could use it for gaming. Or whatever."

"Or whatever," I said. "Any chance I could talk to him?"

"Probably not."

"Why not?"

"He's not available right now."

"OK. When might he become available?"

"Not for a while," Brenda said. "He's in jail."

I GLANCED DOWN AT her granddaughter, realized that she'd nodded off and her head was now tilted against my left arm.

"Jail," I said.

"Drunken driving," Brenda said.

"When was he arrested?"

"Few nights back," Brenda said. "Having a little difficulty making bond at the moment. But soon."

"Do you happen to have keys to his place?"

"His place? You mean his room upstairs?"

"Is that where the laptop is?"

She shook her head.

"Then where?"

"I don't know. I wouldn't tell you if I did, but I really don't. He's got it somewhere."

"Any chance you could ask him? He gets visitors, right?"

Without answering my question, she said, "Why did you say you want this laptop again?"

"There's files on it I need."

"What kind of files."

"Important ones."

"You got any money?"

"I'm sorry?"

"If the files are so important, they must be worth something."

"They might," I said.

"Tell you what. You give me the money to get Dave out of jail, I'll ask him where it is."

"What's his bond?"

"Thousand. Ten percent on ten-thousand surety."

"Seems high for a DUI."

"Third one."

"Does he have a lawyer?"

"Not yet."

"How do I know you'll ask him if I get you the money?"

"You'll know because I said I would," Brenda said.

For just a moment I pondered how far the laptop had moved in such a short time, from a conference room at Fletcher's nursing home to tony Upper Arlington and manicured New

Albany to the grit of Mary Miller's northside apartment to the rough neighborhoods of the Hilltop. Yet despite my tour of Columbus I felt no closer to regaining it than the night Reilly beat me unconscious.

"All right," I said. "I know a couple bail bondsmen. You'll have to give me a while. Few hours."

"Can't you just give me the money?" Brenda said.

"No."

"How do I know I can trust you?"

"Trust me?"

"Yeah—that you'll do it."

"I said I would. Just like you said you'll ask Dave where the laptop is."

Brenda laughed. A long, hoarse, rough cackle.

"What," I said.

"It's just so fucking rich," she said.

"What?"

"You."

"What about me?" I said, getting impatient.

"Woody Fucking Hayes," she said. "Man of honor."

# 27

IT WAS CLOSER TO LUNCHTIME THAN NOT, and since I was in the neighborhood I decided to pay Roy a visit. His church ran a soup kitchen and clothes distribution center off Grubb Street in the Bottoms, a blighted neighborhood along West Broad Street that made the Hilltop look like Scarsdale. When I arrived he was lugging a black plastic bag he'd pulled from the used clothes drop-off bin.

"Check this out," he said, removing two full-size maize-and-blue University of Michigan winter coats.

"You got a license for that kind of contraband?"

"Sad thing is, even I'll have a hard time giving them away."

Inside, I caught him up on the case while I stood behind the counter ladling mashed potatoes and Salisbury steak and canned green beans onto Styrofoam plates as people shuffled in front of me. You worked for food at Roy's on a rotating basis through the week, no exceptions.

"Hold on a second," Roy said, after I explained my meeting at Wendy's the afternoon before. "Her name is Anne. *Anne?*"

"That's right. So what?"

"Woody and Anne," Roy said. "Don't you get it? Like Woody and Anne Hayes. It's just too cute."

"First of all," I said, "my name is Andy, not Woody. Second of all, it's nothing like that. She's practically a client."

"Are you charging her?"

"No."

"Did you not just tell me you thought about asking her to dinner?"

"Yes, but—"

"No buts allowed in love or war," Roy said. "And I've got plenty of experience in both."

"Why do you always do this?" I said.

"Do what?"

"Read things into my encounters with women."

"Because I know you."

"Like hell you do."

"Sure I do. You're an uxorious fellow, through and through. You just haven't found the right uxor yet."

"Uxorious," I said.

"Excessively doting on one's wife—"

"I know what uxorious means," I said. "And I've got two divorces and a broken engagement to prove I'm nothing of the sort."

"Nothing of the sort, yet," Roy said.

I dug up a scoop of mashed potatoes and put it on the out-reached plate before me. I looked up and saw the woman from Roy's church van the other night.

"Theresa," I said. "Isn't it?"

"Yeah."

"Do you remember me?"

"Yeah."

"You still listening to Roy?"

She leaned forward. Her eyes were watery and red. There was alcohol on her breath. Roy wouldn't let raging drunks in, but he tried to be flexible. Wouldn't have any parishioners otherwise, was his reasoning.

She said, "I could really use a cigarette."

"Can't help you," I said.

"Blow job," she said. "Ten bucks. Out back. Five minutes."

"Still can't help you," I said. I set a piece of steak on her plate. "Keep listening to Roy, OK?"

"Yeah."

I turned to Roy as she moved down the serving line, toward the cookies.

I said, "I'm not sure you're getting through to her."

"At least she's here and not out there," he added, nodded toward the street. "Baby steps."

BACK HOME, I TRIED to sort things out. Coming up with $1,000 wasn't going to be easy. I thought briefly about tapping Burke, who could have dipped into his pocket without a second thought to make it happen. But I didn't want to cross that line yet, especially after our conversation about Special Agent Morris. I got on the computer and tapped into my various bank accounts. With a squeeze here and a squeeze there, and dipping too far down into petty cash, and calling in one small favor from a bail bondsman I knew, I could pull it off. But it was going to be close. I called the cell phone number Brenda had given me and told her to meet me on Mound Street around the corner from the jail at 4 p.m.

Next, I thought about what Brenda had told me about Reilly. He'd worked for the state at one point. As a youth prison guard. God help the kids at that center, I thought. I got on the phone, and spent the next couple of hours getting bounced between the Department of Youth Services and the agency that administers all state employee matters as I tried to run down Reilly's personnel file.

Despite some relatively cooperative people at both agencies, it was clear by three o'clock that I wasn't getting the records today. To change things up I made calls to the Department of Rehabilitation and Correction to check on the other thing Brenda had mentioned, that Reilly had supposedly traded up from guard to inmate. I went through the same drill, and soon determined that it would take at least a day for that info as well.

At five minutes after 4 p.m. I parked a block up from Barry's Bonds, fed three quarters into the meter, then walked over to the storefront office where Brenda was waiting.

"About time," she said.

I ignored her and held open the door.

Like every other business in Columbus, Barry O'Brien proudly displayed his Ohio State sports memorabilia. The only difference was that his mementoes consisted of a wall full of mug shots of various Buckeye football and basketball players his office had helped spring over the years.

"I really wish you'd take that down," I said, as I looked up at my own booking photo. "Or at least use a more flattering portrait."

"I'll keep that in mind," Barry said. "Soon as the next time you require my services."

"Very funny," I said. "Dave Brown. I called about him earlier."

"Dave Brown," Barry said. "Bit of bad news there."

"What?" Brenda said.

"He's got a hold on him. Out of Madison County. Driving without insurance. Bond him out here, he goes straight over there."

"That was a mistake," Brenda said. "They were supposed to drop that one. He just didn't have the paper with him. He's got it. Swear."

"Lots of mistakes," Barry said. "Lots of mistakes."

"I talked to the police about it," Brenda protested. "They said they'd drop it."

I said, skeptically, "Did they say when?"

"Supposed to be this week."

"Didn't think that was worth mentioning earlier? That why you just wanted the thousand bucks? Because you knew he was stuck no matter what and you figured, just pocket the cash?"

"I didn't know about no hold," Brenda said.

"Excuse me a minute," I said to Barry, and gestured to Brenda to follow me to the corner of the office.

"We had a deal," I said. "I get Dave out, you ask him where the laptop is."

"He ain't out yet," Brenda said.

"You didn't mention Madison County. You really think they're going to drop a charge like that?"

"I'm telling you, that's what they said. They just have to see the paperwork."

"You've shown it to them?"

"I'm going to."

"When?"

"Was going to do it today."

"Why didn't you?"

"Low on gas money," Brenda said.

I was about to make an impolitic remark when my cell phone buzzed. I looked down. A text from Anne. *You around tonight? Time to talk?*

I thought about Roy. I thought about her green eyes. I thought how sick and tired I was of trying to get the laptop back.

"OK," I said. "Tell you what."

We left Barry's and I had Brenda meet me around the corner at a Shell station, where I filled up her tank. I wasn't sure how much of anything I believed about this business in Madison County, but this much was true: Brenda's late-model Chevy sedan was running on fumes.

# 28

TWO HOURS LATER I WAS SITTING ACROSS
the table from Anne Cooper at Schmidt's off Kossuth in German Village. We'd helped ourselves to the buffet and were
each having a St. Pauli Girl.

This time I hadn't hesitated about inviting her out to eat.
I reasoned: she's the one who had suggested a meeting, and it
was nearly dinnertime by the time we could get together.

"I haven't been here for years," Anne said, slicing into a
Bahama Mama sausage. "It hasn't changed a bit."

"I know what you mean," I said. "Except I haven't been
here for days, or possibly a week. Or two."

She laughed. "Amelia would like it here."

"Your daughter?"

She nodded.

"My sons like it too."

"I'm not sure I knew you had kids."

"Haven't been keeping up with my Wikipedia page?"

She looked at me skeptically.

"Check it out sometime," I said. "It's got everything I don't want anyone to know." I took a gulp of beer. "Anyway—you texted. Something up?"

"I'm worried. About Doug. He keeps asking me if I've found it. The laptop."

"And what do you keep telling him?"

"Like you said. That it's getting closer."

"And what's he say to that?"

"Not much. Just keeps mentioning the files."

"And he never said what they are?"

She shook her head. "'Really important.' That's it."

"Any guesses?"

"None," she said. "He didn't really talk about the business. You told me more about it yesterday than he did in a month."

I took another bite of sausage, added some vinegary potato salad. Chewed. Stepped out on a limb.

"Possible it could be something not quite kosher."

"Like what?"

"I don't know. Something off the books."

"Off the books. You mean illegal?"

I wondered how much weight this particular limb would support. Knew there was only one way to find out.

I said, "The FBI has been looking at Doug. Did you know that?"

She put down her own second forkful of Bahama Mama. "The FBI?"

"I'll take that as a no."

"He never mentioned anything like that. Looking at him for what?"

"I'm not sure," I said. "But it's not about the curtains at his office."

"How do you know that? About the FBI?"

"They talked to me, too."

"When?"

I gave her the *Reader's Digest* version of my meeting with Special Agent Morris.

After a minute, she said, "So not only have you gotten beaten up because of my laptop, the FBI is after you?"

"I'm grateful for your concern," I said. "But don't make it about me."

"Fine," she said. "Then what about me? Suddenly it seems like committing academic fraud is the least of my worries. Or Doug? What about him?"

"I just thought you should know what's going on here. So you'd understand why Doug is so, what's the word you used? Despondent? I wish I knew more, believe me. It might help me figure out how one laptop could cause so much trouble. It's like the Archduke Ferdinand of portable computers."

She snorted. Score one for the private dick.

She took another bite, and then said, "If you don't mind me asking, how is it going? For real?"

I told her about Brenda and the trip to the jail. It was more than the *Reader's Digest* version, but it was still abridged. I left out everything about Reilly and his job and his prison time.

"Back to square one," she said.

"Excuse me?"

"All my fault. Everything. Taking the job. Things with Doug." Her hand moved unconsciously to her scar, then dropped to her side. "Everything."

"Listen," I said. "It's not—"

"No, it's true. I violated the most fundamental principle of my profession by writing those papers. Then I had an affair with a married man. I've gotten you beaten up, possibly twice."

"Anything else?"

"Turns out I probably won't win mother of the year award."

"And I thought that was my department," I said. She looked at me quizzically. "Father of the year," I explained. "I had it sewn up until the police interrupted my hockey outing with the boys to inform me I was a person of interest in a murder." I held up my forefinger and thumb. "So close."

She laughed.

"I'm sorry," she said. "It's just how I get."

I said, "Do you remember yesterday? When we were talking about how I met with Doug? How I ended up getting the laptop in the first place?"

She nodded. "The Wi-Fi at the mall. The porn."

"Something dumb."

She nodded.

"It was a lot worse than dumb," I said. Leaving several details out, including Ted Hamilton's name, I told her what Pete had really done.

"Shit," she said when I was finished.

"I know."

"That's horrible."

"It is horrible. But that's not why I told you."

"Then why?"

"A minute ago, you thought I was going to say something like, 'It's not your fault.' Right?"

"True."

"I'm not going to say that, because you've already admitted you made a couple of mistakes. That doesn't matter to me."

"Says the guy who got attacked with a baseball bat because of me."

"Because of a guy named Danny Reilly," I said. "But more to the point, maybe, also because a kid named Pete Freeley tried to extort a guy with a compromising video that could ruin the guy's life. I mean, *ruin* it. For a lousy thousand bucks. You want to shoulder some blame in this? Fine. But you can just as easily point the finger at Pete."

"So I'm not just an adjunct professor. I'm an adjunct screw-up."

This time it was my turn to laugh.

"Maybe I'm just immune," I said.

"Immune?"

"When you've screwed up as badly as I have, it's easier to overlook other people's mistakes."

AFTER DINNER WE SPLIT a Schmidt's cream puff and had some coffee. We were walking out the door, onto the brick street, when her cell phone made the "Wookie" sound.

"My mom," she said, glancing at the message. "Amelia's not feeling well. I should go."

"That's OK," I said. "I'm pretty much out of clues for the day."

I walked her to her car. It had started raining, and the temperature had dropped.

"Thanks for meeting with me," she said. She put her hand out. It was firm, and warm. I shook it.

"You're welcome," I said. "I'll let you know what happens tomorrow. With the jailbird."

"Thanks," she said.

I was walking away when she called my name.

"Yes?"

"Thank you for everything. I mean it. I promise I won't screw anything else up."

"You can do anything you want, as long as it doesn't result in my head meeting any more baseball bats."

"Good night, then."

"Night."

As I walked away from Schmidt's, up the dark, glistening bricked street toward my house, I thought about Roy. His teasing earlier in the day, at the soup kitchen. Woody and Anne.

I'd have a lot of explaining to do if he caught wind of this meeting.

# 29

GETTING BACK IN TOUCH WITH DOUG
Freeley was at the top of my priority list, especially after my
conversations with Anne. But first I had to follow up on the
information about where Reilly had been working that I'd
wrung out of Watkins, the construction foreman. Imagine
my surprise when I plugged the address into my GPS the next
morning and saw that I'd be going to a house next door to
Doug and Beth's.

After ringing the bell and hearing a rich gong inside, I
waited a couple of minutes before the door was opened by a
dark-haired woman in spandex shorts and a purple workout
bra, her face shiny with perspiration.

"Well, hello there," she said.

I introduced myself and handed her my card.

"Private investigator," she said. "You don't see that a lot
around here. You have something juicy to tell me about my
husband?"

I smiled uneasily. I was not used to having mansion doors
answered by pretty women in purple sports bras.

"Not today," I said.

"Too bad," she said. "Danielle Hastings." She put out her hand. I took it; it was warm and slightly moist. Despite the sheen of sweat on her face, a hint of flowery perfume clung to her. Nice smelling—something lilac-y. "Care to come inside?"

"That's all right," I said. "This will only take a minute."

"Well, I care. I don't feel like standing here in my underwear." She turned and disappeared inside, leaving me no choice. We walked through a vestibule, in and out of a great room and into a kitchen with a copper-topped island that looked about as long as my Odyssey. She poured us both glasses of water from the dispenser on the front of a restaurant-grade brushed-steel refrigerator.

She set down her water, cocked her left hand on her hip, and held my card in the other. "So how can I help you, Mr. Andy Hayes?"

I said, "I'm trying to get some information about a man who worked here a few weeks ago. On your addition." I nodded vaguely in the direction of the back of the house.

"Any man in particular?"

"His name was Danny Reilly." I described him.

"I remember the tattoo," she said. "Who wouldn't? Is he in trouble?"

"Unfortunately, he's dead."

"How awful," she said as though it didn't sound awful at all. "What happened?"

"Someone shot him and dumped him in Grandview Yard quarry."

She wrinkled her nose as if I'd just told an off-color joke.

I said, "I'm wondering if you talked to him at all. If he said or did anything unusual."

"I'm not used to talking to strange men in my house, Andy," she said, emphasizing my name as she said it. "Though I do make exceptions."

"I'm sure you do," I said. "Anything you might have noticed about him? Anything that stood out?"

"The tattoo, obviously. I remember asking if he played football and he just laughed. How about you?"

"Me?"

"Did you play football? You're quite a big guy."

"A bit, back in the day," I said, not sure if she knew who I was and was teasing me or was just flirting with me straight up. Either way, despite her shapely form and large brown eyes, I wanted to end this interview quickly.

"I bet you did," she said. "Want to see my workout room? I'd be curious of your professional opinion. As an athlete, I mean. It's right downstairs."

"Another time, maybe," I said. "I'm sure it's nice."

"You're right," she said. "Very nice."

I put my water down on the top of the island. "So nothing else about Danny?"

"Who?"

"Danny Reilly. The guy who worked on your house."

"No," she said. "Nothing else."

"Well," I said. "Thanks for your help."

"Sure I can't show you my workout room?"

"I'm sure," I said, aware that if I didn't get out of the house soon I wasn't going to be so sure.

"Suit yourself," she said.

I was almost at the door when I had a thought and stopped.

"Do you know Beth Freeley?"

"Beth? My neighbor?"

"That's right."

"I know her, sure. Why? Are you visiting all the ladies on the street today?"

"Maybe I am," I said. "You're not the only one with a workout room, you know."

"Is that right?" Danielle said, her eyes flashing a bit of anger. "And you're suddenly the expert on this?"

"What's it to you?"

"I'll tell you one thing," she said. "Beth isn't the queen of perfection she seems to be."

"Why do you say that?"

"This guy you're talking about? Reilly? Scum. Absolute scum. Disgusting. Not just the tattoo. Language, chewing tobacco, nose picking. The whole nine yards."

"You seem to remember him pretty well now."

"I remember pigs who come into my house," she said. "But the thing is, Beth knew him."

"She knew him? What do you mean?"

"It was about a month ago. I was outside, just coming back from my jog."

"OK."

"She was coming out of her house, and for just a minute we chatted. And that's when it happened."

"What?"

"This guy, Reilly, pulls up in front. He was early, I guess. There was a crew of three or four guys working on our addition. He was low on the totem pole, far as I could tell."

"All right."

"He gets out of the car and stares at us. No surprise there. But then I notice he's looking at Beth real hard. I was about to say something to her when she looked in his direction, and she goes absolutely white. I mean, just like in the movies. I'd never seen anything like it."

"Like what?"

"Like she'd seen a ghost."

"Did you say anything to her?"

"I might have. 'Are you all right?' Something like that."

"What'd she say?"

"Nothing. She just excused herself real fast. Walked across the lawn and into her house. Didn't look back at him, didn't look back at me."

"Did Reilly do anything after that?"

"I could see him looking at her house real carefully. Then after a minute he looked back at me. Not in a way that made me comfortable. So I went inside."

"How long was he here? Working on your addition, I mean."

"Another week or so."

"Did he ever talk to Beth? Go over there?"

"Not that I could see."

"Did he ever come back after that? After the work was done?"

"Couldn't say. Lot of people coming and going around here. Lots of construction."

I thought about this. It seemed a truly bizarre coincidence that Reilly had been working on a house right next to Beth. The fact that they might have recognized each other was an even stranger turn of events.

"Thanks," I said. "That was helpful."

"Anytime," she said. "Glad I could finally be of some use to you."

I let the remark go. If I'd had any desire to see Danielle Hastings's workout room, it had been doused by her description of Danny Reilly and her inflection of the word *scum*.

She shut the door behind me, hard, and I walked down the steps. I turned to my left and crossed the yard to the Freeleys'. Only one of the Escalades sat in the drive.

The look I got from Beth when she opened the door was about as far from Danielle's ogling as you could get.

"Doug's not here," she said.

"I figured as much," I said. "Middle of the day and all that. I actually had a question for you."

"What kind of question."

The day had gotten chillier, and I'd left my jacket in the van, but she made no move to open the door wider or invite me in.

"There's this guy," I said, deciding to jump right in. "Danny Reilly. He beat me up, stole the laptop with the video on it. *Pete's* video. And now he's dead."

"I'm sorry to hear that," she said.

"And here's the funny thing. I was looking into his background a little bit, and I found out he worked construction. And wouldn't you know, he was working right next door a few weeks back." I nodded in the direction of Danielle's house.

"How odd," she said, her voice the slightest bit sharp.

"It just seems like a big coincidence," I said.

"You said you had a question."

"Thing is, I'm just wondering if you knew him."

"Knew him?"

"That's right."

She shook her head. "No. I didn't."

"Are you sure? Seems odd that a guy who beat me up for a laptop that had videos your son put on there happened to work construction next door."

For no more than three seconds, Beth didn't say anything. I tried to read her face, but it was blank. Then she said, "It does seem odd. And I'm sorry you got beat up. And I guess I'm also sorry he's dead, even though I have no idea who he is. But it's just a coincidence. Columbus is a small place. You know that. Things can happen."

"Columbus isn't that small. Twice as big as Cleveland, last time I checked."

"What's your point?"

"That seems too big for a coincidence."

"I suppose," she said. "If you're the kind of person who keeps track of things like that."

"I'm not a big fan of coincidences," I said.

"It's a busy day for me," she said after a minute. Her eyes drifted past me to the street. I turned and saw a red Dodge Durango pull into her drive. Two women got out, waved toward Beth.

"Expecting company?"

"I have a makeup business. They're clients. That all right with you?"

"Of course," I said. "Just curious."

"I really need to go. Was there anything else?"

I considered the question. She could well be telling the truth. Maybe she had nothing to do with Danny Reilly. Or if she didn't know Reilly, someone in her family did. Pete? Who had a really good reason to get the laptop back. Doug? A guy who needed those files so badly. Or was there another possibility: that Reilly sought them out for some reason. That they didn't know him, at least not at first, but that he'd chosen them. Was he working for someone else? Fletcher? Or Ted Hamilton? Was it possible my original client was doing an end run around me in his desperation to retrieve the incriminating video of him and Jennifer Rawlings?

Except there was that little tidbit from Danielle. *She goes absolutely white. Just like in the movies.*

"Mr. Hayes?" Beth said. "I really need for you to go."

The two women had arrived at the steps. They eyed me curiously.

I considered making a covering remark about mascara for my wife. But then a twinge of pain went through me knee, a leftover gift from Reilly.

"Nothing else," I said. "Have a nice day."

# 30

I GLANCED AT MY WATCH AS I DROVE BACK up Greensward Road. I had a couple of hours before my appointment with Honey Huntington. It would be tight, but I knew what I had to do. And I knew a phone call wasn't going to cut it.

American Financial Health Care occupied three floors of a glassed corporate office building off Metro Place in Dublin, reached via a series of winding boulevards running past dressed up drainage ponds that even now, in mid-November, sported a number of large Canada geese. It's close to being on the other side of Columbus from New Albany, but sure enough, it took me just twenty minutes to get there.

After getting off on the seventh floor I walked over to the company's glass doors, pulled them open and walked into a lobby that was decidedly empty. As was the receptionist's desk and the darkened conference room behind it, though I couldn't help noticing the boxes stacked along a far wall.

"Hello?" I said.

No answer. I heard someone's voice down the hall and turned in that direction. The first office I came to, on the right, was also empty, as if never occupied. The second, on the left, looked as if someone still worked there, but the light was off and I got the feeling no one had sat in that chair for a while. I proceeded down the hall and came to the corner office. Freeley was inside, on the phone. His eyes opened wide when he saw me at the door. He wrapped up his conversation quickly and hung up.

"Andy?" he said. "What are you doing here?" Then he brightened. "Do you have the laptop?"

"Not yet."

"Then why are you here?"

"Just came by to talk."

"Talk?"

"Chat," I said. "About you. And Anne Cooper."

FREELEY SAT SLUMPED IN his chair. Stacked boxes climbed up the rear wall of his office past waist level. His desk was a morass of paper, covering almost every free inch of space and threatening to cascade off. I counted thirteen sticky notes jutting off the four sides of his computer monitor. I was standing because the chair where I might have sat was stacked high with file folders.

"Anne's a nice girl," he said. "I'm sorry she got involved in this."

"Involved in what?"

"This whole thing. With Pete. And the laptop. And my files."

"Time out," I said. "You put those files on her laptop when you realized she'd brought it with her. Made up a story about a broken DVD player. And you're sorry she, quote, got involved?"

"I know how it sounds," he said.

"Beth know about her?"

Doug nodded. "She has every reason to leave, or kick me out. But all she says is to get the laptop back. Says we can start over after that."

"Start over?"

"That's right."

"Forgiving woman."

"Amazing woman. Doesn't deserve me."

Maybe I'm jaded, but the look on Freeley's face didn't quite match the words coming from his mouth.

"How long have you been married?"

He thought about it. "Eighteen years, next month."

I made a quick calculation. "You had Pete pretty quickly," I said. "Or was he an early wedding present?"

"That'd be none of your damn business."

"Wrong," I said. "If you want your precious laptop back, it's all my business now."

"Look, I just don't see—"

"How'd you meet?"

"Meet?"

"You and Beth."

"Why the hell should I tell you that?"

"It's my business now, like I said. Try to keep your eyes on the prize."

"You've got a hell of a lot of nerve."

"Flattery will get you everywhere. I'm waiting."

"We met here," he said after a minute.

"Here?"

"At the office. She was a temporary secretary. We were a lot smaller then, business was booming. We needed help. She came in and we hit it off right away."

"I bet you did."

"What's that supposed to mean?"

"Nothing. You're from Columbus?"

He shook his head. "Cleveland."

"Beth?"

"From here. Columbus."

"She have family here still?"

"For Chrissake. What does that have to do with the laptop?"

"I don't know, exactly. Humor me."

"I'm tired of playing games with you."

"Me too, trust me. Which is why I'm trying to help you."

"Big help."

"Listen," I said. "Just work with me, OK? Ten minutes. Then I'm gone, trying to get what we both want back."

He looked at me. I noticed dark circles under his eyes.

"Fine," he said. "Fucking fine. Just get it over with."

"Beth," I said. "Family here?"

"No," Freeley said. "No family. She was an only child, and her parents were killed in a car crash long before we met."

"I'm sorry."

"Yes," he said. "Terrible thing."

"How long have you lived in New Albany?"

"We moved in ten years ago. And to answer your next question, we lived in Westerville before that."

"You moved from Westerville to New Albany?" The northeast-side community was a destination move for a lot of families, usually out of Columbus. It had recently been voted one of the top ten suburbs in the country, if you cared about those kinds of things.

"The school district was having some financial problems. A levy had failed. Beth was worried about the schools. For Pete."

"But not you?"

"I liked our place in Westerville." Then he added, quickly: "And I like our place now."

"Must be expensive, though."

"I beg your pardon?"

"I mean, compared to Westerville. Big house, big cars. Those taxes."

"What's your point?"

"No point, really. Just guessing you're a guy with a lot of obligations. And also guessing Beth's home makeup business doesn't quite cover everything."

"How do you know what she does?"

"She told me. Couple hours ago."

"You talked to Beth?"

"I was at your house. She didn't tell you I'd been there?"

"You were at our house? Why?"

"I went to see one of your neighbors. Stopped by afterward."

"Why?"

"Name Danny Reilly mean anything to you?"

"No," he said. "Should it?"

"He's the guy that took the laptop. Beat me up for it. Not long after I talked to you and Beth. Then somebody put a bullet in him and pushed him into Grandview Yard quarry."

"Jesus," he said. "Do they know who did it?"

"Someone with a gun," I said. "Here's the odd thing: he worked construction, and one of his jobs was at your neighbor's house. Danielle Hastings? Few weeks back."

"You're kidding."

"Wish I were. Seems like a strange coincidence."

"I guess. You could have told me you'd talked to Beth."

"I'm telling you now."

"You ask Beth? About this Reilly guy?"

"She said she didn't know him."

"You sound like you don't believe her."

"I just think it's odd, is all," I said. "I meet the two of you, then the same night a guy who was doing construction next door beats me up and steals the laptop. And now he's dead."

"And you're thinking we had something to do with that? Are you out of your mind?"

"You have to admit it's odd."

"I don't have to admit anything."

"You know," I said, deciding it was time to change the subject. "I can't help but notice your office looks like it's two days past the fire sale. Everything OK here?"

"Yes," he said quickly. "We're reorganizing. It's a little chaotic right now."

"Where is everybody?"

"Everybody?"

"All the other employees."

"The other suites," he said vaguely, waving his hand in a way that I took to be a reference to upper floors.

"Feels lonely," I said.

"Look, I've really got to get some things done. Are we finished?"

"Almost. So you don't know why Danny Reilly, who was working construction right next to your house, might have taken the laptop from me and then ended up dead?"

"I don't know anything about any of that. I agree it sounds strange. But I'm telling you the truth."

"If you had told me the truth before, about you and Anne, it might have helped speed things along."

"Sure," he said. "Just blurted it out in my living room in front of Beth."

"You had my number," I said. "You called to set up the meeting."

"I'm sorry," he said. "It didn't cross my mind to tell you about an ill-advised affair I was having that could very well destroy my marriage. Satisfied?"

"Anne says you're despondent about the laptop. That you're desperate to get it back."

"Anne told you that?"

"Are you?"

"What?"

"Despondent?"

"I need that laptop returned," he said slowly. "Will I be upset until Anne gets it and I know those files are safe? Yes."

"You know," I said. "It occurs to me that these offices are kind of isolated up here. So few people."

"I already told you—"

"Keep a gun handy, by any chance? For protection?"

"A gun? What are you talking about?"

"I'm just wondering how desperate you might be. To get the laptop back."

"Jesus Christ," Freeley said. "You think I shot this guy? This guy I don't even know?"

"I don't think anything," I said. "It was just a question."

"Time's up," Freeley said. "Get the hell out of here."

I might have decided to stay, except I happened to glance at the clock on his wall just then and saw it was the wrong side of 11:30 a.m. and I was due on Honey Huntington's street soon.

I leaned forward, a little closer to Freeley.

"Anything else you haven't told me? Any other details that slipped your mind? Let me know, all right?"

"Please leave," Freeley said wearily.

"I'll be in touch," I said, and strolled back down the hall toward the receptionist's desk.

Riding the elevator down, I tried to figure out what, if anything, I'd learned. I couldn't decide if I believed Freeley when he said he didn't know Reilly. I was sure I didn't believe that line about his office reorganizing. But it wasn't until I was outside and walking to my van that I thought of one reason dropping by in person had been useful. Nowhere in Freeley's office, on the walls or the desk or the window shelf, had I spied a single picture of his wife or son.

# 31

MY INVESTIGATION INTO THE MEANDERINGS OF
Honey Huntington had reached the money shot phase. She and
her lady friend met at the North Market again, and I snapped
a couple of decent photos as they exchanged air kisses in the
parking lot. I didn't bother following them inside, since I had
their routine down pat. I knew I had approximately forty-five
minutes to kill until they re-emerged and headed to Banninger's
Buttons for what I assumed was more than button shopping.

In the meantime I called a series of state telephone numbers for updates on Reilly's personnel file and prison records.
I left two voicemails and spoke to a third person who wasn't
familiar with my request but said she'd look into it. I knew it
was also time to probe deeper into the backgrounds of Doug
and Beth Freeley, but that was more than my smart phone
could handle.

I was checking my e-mail for the fifth time when I saw a
new message from the Department of Rehabilitation and Correction pop up. Almost simultaneously, Honey and her friend
walked out of the market and started strolling toward High

Street. Keeping a careful eye on them, I got out of the van and began my tail as I read the results of my request. Brenda Brown hadn't been too far off the mark. Reilly had been imprisoned almost twenty years ago for drug possession, drug distribution, and conveyance of contraband. A second stint, for receiving stolen property and theft seven years later. A third visit, for burglary and receiving stolen property, that ended two years ago. So Reilly had been a frequent flyer in the state prison system. That didn't really tell me a whole lot more than I already knew, or could have guessed. Reilly was a badass, and had been that way for a while. And like a good percentage of badasses, he had ended up dead.

I exited my e-mail and concentrated on Honey and friend. I used the phone's camera to get a couple more shots of them from behind. They weren't great, but no matter: I had the photos from the parking lot, and the only other picture that really mattered today, the money shot, would be them entering the button store together.

They were a couple blocks from Banninger's when my phone went off.

"Andy, it's Kevin Harding."

"No comment."

"You have a second?"

"I might have to sign off suddenly. What's up?"

"You asked me about Ted Hamilton."

"That's right."

"I checked around. Talked to our Statehouse guys, plus a couple people I know in the Legislature."

"Appreciate it."

"I don't know what Hamilton told you, but if he's been having an affair, it's hardly his first."

"Oh?" I remembered I'd been careful not to tell Harding about the full circumstances of Hamilton's case. But I started to pay more attention.

"It's also hardly his second, third, or fourth, if you catch my drift."

"Eye for the ladies, I take it?"

"Both eyes, to say the least. Prefers the younger aides, which as you can imagine the Statehouse is full of. Typical scenario is meeting them in the course of lobbying a lawmaker. He's got the money to wine and dine them."

"Tale as old as time?"

"Mostly."

"Mostly?"

"Feeling is he's using a lot of the girls. Gets them to persuade the people they work for to look favorably on one of his bills."

Ahead of me, Honey's friend stopped and looked into a window of a vintage secondhand clothes shop. As she did, Honey's left hand drifted casually across her friend's back, and further down, and even further down, then back up to hold her hand. A squeeze, just for a moment. But still. Shit. Would have made a nice couple of pictures. For the album, you know.

I said, collecting myself, "So these affairs are common knowledge."

"Yes and no."

"Meaning?"

"He's discreet. People I talked to said there were always rumors but not a lot of proof. But that's true of just about everyone over there."

"So how do you know any of it's true? He wouldn't be the first man to get by on innuendo."

"I wondered the same thing. But somebody I know suggested I check the divorce records."

"He was married before?"

"Not as far as I know. His wife filed for divorce after one of his flings apparently went a little public. She showed up at his house—the girlfriend, I mean. I read some of the filings. It wasn't pretty. Turns out she, I mean the other woman, accused him of stepping out on *her* with a someone else who also wasn't his wife."

"Who was she? The girlfriend, I mean."

"Emily Goodwin."

"Should I know her?"

"Probably not. She was somebody's L.A."

"L.A.?"

"Legislative aide."

"So what happened?"

"His wife withdrew the petition. They reconciled. Not everybody who starts a divorce finishes one."

"I'll have to take your word for that. What happened to Emily?"

Honey and her friend were now almost to the button shop. Their heads were close together in conversation. I stepped up the pace.

"That's the sad thing," Harding said. "She committed suicide two weeks after showing up at his house."

"She killed herself?"

"Apparently."

"What's that supposed to mean?"

"Everything pointed that way. There was a note, and other circumstances."

"Circumstances?"

"Financial problems. And a history of mental illness. But you know how it is."

"How what is?"

"Drownings. Always tough to call."

"She drowned?"

Honey and her friend were at the shop now, looking at a display in the window and laughing. They'd linked arms.

"Drowned herself. Common with women. I see them on police reports all the time."

"Where?"

"Everywhere. Columbus, Delaware, Chillicothe."

"No," I said impatiently. "Where did she drown herself?"

Their voices descending to a giggle, Honey and her friend opened the door and went inside. Crap, I thought.

"Grandview Yard quarry," Harding said. "Threw herself over the edge."

TEN MINUTES LATER, I was in my van and headed down High Street faster than I should have been driving. As I sped along, my phone rang again. Caller blocked.

"It's Henry Fielding," the detective said.

"I'm a little busy right now," I said.

"That's handy, since you're about to be a lot busier. I need you in my office five minutes ago."

"I'm in the middle of something."

"Drop it."

"No," I said.

"Don't push it, Hayes."

"What's so urgent it can't wait an hour?"

"I'm not answering questions. I'm telling you to get down here. Now."

"And I'm telling you I'm in the middle of something and I'll get there when I can."

"You aren't here in fifteen minutes, I'm booking your ass in jail the moment you walk in."

"Now there's an incentive for me to come by."

"Damn it, Hayes. Quit screwing around."

"All I know how to do," I said, and cut the connection.

The phone started ringing not twenty seconds later, just as I passed Nationwide Insurance headquarters and its gardens and pools stretching down High Street. I let it ring. Like I said, I was in the middle of something.

TED HAMILTON'S OFFICE WAS around the corner from the Capitol on State Street in a nondescript building between the old downtown post office—it now housed a law firm—and a Schoedinger funeral home. As I got off the elevator on the second floor I was greeted by a youngish-looking blonde sitting at a mahogany desk on a thick red carpet surrounded by gleaming wood-paneled walls.

"Mr. Hamilton's not in," she said blankly, in response to my query. "Was he expecting you?"

"I believe he was, yes."

She moved her computer mouse, tapped on some keys, then frowned. "I don't see anything on his calendar, Mr. . . . ?"

"Hayes," I said. "Andy Hayes."

She played with her computer again. "I'm sorry. Would you like to schedule an appointment?"

"I need to see him right away."

"That's not possible."

"Maybe I could go meet up with him."

She frowned. "He's with a client, I believe."

"Maybe I could help him with his client."

"I don't think so," she managed to say.

There was a leather couch on the other side of the lobby. I walked over to it and sat down. A glass-topped coffee table in front of it was covered with old issues of *Governing* magazine.

The receptionist said, "I don't believe he's expected anytime soon."

"That's OK," I said. "I just wanted someplace comfortable to sit while I called him."

Hamilton answered on the third ring.

"Andy Hayes," I said. "We need to talk."

"Happy to. What's a good time?"

"Right now."

"Right now's not great. Couple hours maybe?"

I stood up and walked back to the receptionist's desk. As I did, I put my phone on speaker mode. "Ted?" I said.

"Still here."

"I'm here in the lobby of your office. With, ah." I looked inquiringly at the woman.

"Brooke," she said, the frost in her voice matching her hair.

"Brooke," I repeated. I looked at her. "Can you hear Ted all right?" She stared icily at me.

"So anyway," I continued. "If you can't meet me right now, maybe we could go over your case on the phone. Names and details, that kind of thing. I'll keep it hands free so I can take some notes."

There was a long pause. Then I heard him say, "Take it off speaker."

"All right," I said. But I waited until I'd walked back to the couch and sat down again.

"What the hell is this?" Hamilton said.

"Where are you?"

"I'm with a client."

"Brooke already informed me of that. I mean, physically, where."

Another pause. Then: "Mitchell's. I'm having some drinks. Then dinner. It's not a good time."

"Mitchell's," I said. "Excellent choice." The downtown steak house was a perennial locale for deal making. "I'll be right there."

"Andy—" he said. But I had already hung up.

I stood up. "Mitchell's," I said to Brooke. "Care to join us?"

"No, thank you," she said, though I could have sworn—it was Mitchell's, after all—that the look in her eyes said differently.

MITCHELL'S WAS A ten-minute walk from State Street, sitting surreptitiously on Third across from the Renaissance

Columbus hotel. Hamilton was at the bar with two heavyset men and one petite-looking woman when I came in, but he stood up immediately and approached me.

"Andy," he said in an unnaturally elevated voice, gripping my hand in a hearty, hail-fellow-well-met fashion. "Good to see you!"

I took his elbow gently, which to judge by the alarm in his eyes wasn't gently enough, and steered him to the opposite end of the bar.

"What's up?" he said loudly in the same friendly voice. Out of the corner of my eye I could see his drinking companions looking curiously in our direction.

"I'll tell you what's up. Emily Goodwin. That's what."

"Emily Goodwin?" His voice dropped as he feigned ignorance.

"Don't play any dumber than you already are. Did it not occur to you to mention you had a track record at this kind of thing?"

"What are you talking about?"

"Preying on young women, that's what. You think for one second I'd have taken your case if I knew you chased skirts as a second career? Or that one of your girlfriends got so upset she jumped into a quarry?"

"Listen—"

"Or maybe she didn't jump. Maybe you pushed her to make sure she wasn't going to be a problem for you anymore. Heck of a thing when your girlfriend shows up at your house and your wife answers the door. Or so I'm told. You can imagine a guy resorting to desperate measures."

"Are you crazy?" he said, an alarmed look on his face. "I had nothing to do with that. Emily was very . . . disturbed. She had a lot of issues. It was a tragedy, but nothing to do with me."

"Other than the part about you sleeping with a young woman with a lot of issues. What were you hoping to get out of it? A bill authorizing more keg sales?"

"You're way over the line here, Andy."

"No, I'm right on the line. And I see it all perfectly. How'd it work? You're in her apartment for one last fling? Type the note on her computer when she's out of the room? Suggest you take a drive together? See the scenery at Grandview Yard? I hear it's a favorite place for lovers."

"Stop it," he said. "That's a bunch of bullshit. Emily has nothing to do with my situation. With the reason I hired you in the first place. Which I thought you said you'd resolved, by the way."

"I had it resolved," I said. "And then it got complicated."

"Complicated?"

"Somebody named Danny Reilly took the laptop and traded me a goose egg for it. Then two days later he gets snagged on a fishing hook in the same quarry as Emily, only he's got a bullet in him. You one of those guys who sticks with what works? What's good for Emily is good for Reilly? That it?"

"You're out of your mind," he said. "I didn't kill Emily Goodwin, and I have no idea who Danny Reilly is."

"Do you have a gun, Ted?"

"That's it," he said, struggling to keep his voice down. "We're done. You're off the case."

"Don't be ridiculous," I said. "It's too late to fire me. This has got a life on its own now."

"I don't care. I'll handle it from now on."

"Ah, that's comforting," I said. "I can only imagine how that will work. Call up Jennifer Rawlings? Offer to take *her* for a ride? Careful, though. Those kinds of girls are usually good swimmers. You might have to pop her in the back of the head. Doesn't get rid of the video, I guess. But at least there's one less witness."

To my surprise—since I'd been mostly bluffing—a look of shock came over Hamilton's face. I realized I'd struck a nerve of some kind. But about what? That he'd actually shot Reilly? Or fantasized about offing Jennifer?

"I didn't kill anybody," he said. "I just want all this to go away."

I stared at him, releasing his elbow as I did. I said, "Since you've lied to me from the beginning, you'll appreciate my unwillingness to believe you. But I'll tell you one thing."

"What."

"You killed Emily Goodwin. No question about it. Maybe you didn't push her into the quarry. Maybe she really did go there by herself. Maybe you were chasing the next cute thing by then. But after what you did to her, knowing the problems she had? Those were your hands on her back all the way down."

He was silent, looking down at the bar.

Then he said, "What do you want me to do?"

"It's real simple," I said, turning to leave. "I want you to stop being a lecherous sack of shit."

# 32

"YOU WANT TO EXPLAIN TO ME"—FIELDING was saying in a voice just above a whisper, which I'd noticed in his case was more effective than yelling—"why the hell the first thing I hear from Brenda Brown when I finally locate her is, 'This other guy was already here'? And this other guy turns out to be you?"

"I never said I was with the police," I said. "Not for a second."

"I'm waiting."

"I've got a case of my own," I said. "I can't help it if it intersects with yours from time to time."

"You can help anything I tell you to," Fielding said. "This is about your missing laptop?"

"That's right."

"The same laptop Danny Reilly lifted from you?"

"Right again."

"And now he's dead, and you're talking to his relatives."

"Trying to get answers for my client."

"And who's that again?"

180

"A private individual. With zero connection to this case."

I thought about Hamilton. Was I absolutely sure about that?

"One more time. Who is it?"

"It's confidential."

"Yeah? Here's what's not confidential. Me charging you with obstruction if I don't get the name in the next ten seconds."

His voice was getting quieter, which I knew was a bad sign.

But I also thought: he doesn't know about Brenda's son. The deal with his bond. Brenda hadn't said anything. Honor among thieves: she didn't want to blow our arrangement. Or more to the point: her access to my wallet.

What would happen if I outed Hamilton? Despite my own suspicions, could I keep him clean in Fielding's eyes long enough to wrap this thing up? The timing was iffy: Barry O'Brien had phoned just as I was walking into the police station to say the hold had been lifted but he had to leave for the day and the earliest I could bond out the son was tomorrow.

"If I tell you who it is," I said, "could you give me a day before you talk to him?"

"Are you bargaining with me? In your position?"

"Simple question."

"Why in the hell would I ever agree to that?"

"I'm not sure," I admitted. "It would make life easier for me, and I think it would actually make things easier for you in the long run."

"What's a day give you?"

I thought, time to get the laptop back, delete Anne's papers, Pete Freeley's video, Doug Freeley's files, then return it to Anne clean, no questions asked.

I said, "A chance to cover up evidence and make it easier for me to get a clean getaway."

"Go to hell, Hayes," Fielding said as he pushed a pad of yellow lined legal paper across his desk. "Write down your client's name. Then write down everybody you've talked to about

Reilly. Explain why. Give me all the information you can about them. Do not pass Go. Do not collect two hundred dollars."

I thought of a million snappy retorts. I knew the detective had nothing on Reilly that he could book me on. But a generic obstruction of justice charge was another thing, even if just for spite. And every minute I cooled my heels in Franklin County Jail was another minute I couldn't spend wrapping this case up once and for all.

I settled for "Yes, sir," and started writing.

I set down Hamilton's problem, but left out Jennifer Rawlings and Pete Freeley. I segued to Doug Freeley but left out Beth Freeley. I mentioned Mary Miller, knowing she was the one person police actually knew about. I gave them Bobby Fletcher's name, but left out Anne. Didn't even bother with Tommy Watkins. I was taking a risk not filling in all the gaps because I could see how pissed Fielding was. But I had no choice. It was going to be a close race—my finish line the laptop, his the entire cast of characters—and I needed every angle possible to cross the line first.

When I was done I pushed the pad back across to him. He studied it carefully.

"This is pretty good," he said. "Who'd you leave out?"

I waited a beat too long and said, "The guy who did it."

"Always the wiseass."

"I try."

"Just not hard enough."

"Don't know about that."

"Oh?"

"You have to wonder."

"Wonder?"

"How come I talked to Brenda Brown first? Where were you? Isn't this your job?"

I was wrong once again. Fielding's voice could go even lower.

# 33

IT WAS PAST FOUR WHEN I GOT HOME.
My headache had returned in Doug's office, gotten worse
talking to Hamilton, and exploded getting grilled by Fielding. There was a good chance I would have limped into bed
instead of plopping down in front of my computer if Henry
Huntington hadn't called just as I walked inside. I gave him
the latest update.

"That's all she does?" he said, a hint of disgust in his
voice. "Shop?"

"Well, lunch, then shop."

I wasn't ready to relay the information about her and her
lady friend just yet. It was not the kind of bomb I usually
dropped on a client over the phone. Plus, technically, he'd asked
me to determine if she was having an affair with another man.

"You're sure she's not meeting someone?"

"Unless you count her girlfriends, yes, I'm sure."

"And her routine's always the same?" he said, as though
offended by Honey's punctuality.

"Like clockwork," I said.

"Well, keep an eye on her. I still have my suspicions."

"Happy to," I lied.

After I hung up I realized something was still nagging at me about this case. Starting with this: I was beginning to sympathize with Honey.

AFTER I HUNG UP I got to work, despite my headache. Fielding had given me no choice: the clock was ticking. I had access to a Nexis account through Burke, and the first thing I did was run Doug's name through it. That gave me his residential history back to a house in the Cleveland suburb of Lakewood more than twenty-five years ago. It also gave me a possible maiden name for Beth—Jones, how helpful—and a much shorter address history. She'd lived at Lakeside Apartments before her address switched to one in Westerville: their first house, as Doug had explained. The county auditor informed me that she and Doug jointly owned the house in New Albany, a steal at $1.3 million. They were married eighteen years ago, just like Doug said. They'd never been arrested, according to municipal court records. Beth, however, had had two separate speeding tickets within the past two years. Nothing too unusual about that—I'd have found my own name more than that if I'd searched for myself—but it was enough for me to fax a request for both Doug's and Beth's driving records to the Bureau of Motor Vehicles. In the meantime I checked my e-mail, called again for Danny Reilly's personnel files—still no luck—and on a whim trolled through the *Dispatch* archives for a couple killed in a car crash twenty years ago or so. Nothing came up, including any obituary that mentioned a daughter named Beth Jones, but that wasn't saying much. Sad to say, there are a lot of double-fatal car crashes.

Shortly before five I took a break by grabbing the leash and heading for the park with Hopalong. When I got back I put water on to boil for pasta and took some of the Carfagna sausage out of the refrigerator to use in spaghetti sauce. I was headed back to the computer for another check of e-mail when my phone went off. It was Anne.

"Hi there," I said, a little too eagerly.

"Hi," she said, her voice sounding small.

"Something wrong?"

"You went to see Doug."

"That's right."

"You told him you knew about us."

"I did," I said slowly.

"I wish you hadn't."

"Why?"

"I just—it feels awkward. You knowing what you know, and then talking to him about it. I'm trying to work this out, and it's just—difficult."

"Did he call you?"

"He texted me. He was angry."

"At you?"

"At me. And at you."

"What'd you tell him?"

"I told him I was sorry."

"Sorry about what?"

"Sorry . . ."

I waited.

"Sorry that I'd talked to you. I mean, about us. Doug and me."

"I'm not sure I understand," I said.

"Understand what?"

"I thought you needed help with your situation. That that's why you stopped me, at Fletcher's."

"I did. I do."

"What happened between you and Doug is part of your problem. Not your relationship, I mean, but what happened at the cabin. The laptop and the files. That's just the reality."

Silence.

"Anne?" I said after several long moments.

"I just feel a little violated, is all," she said.

"Violated?"

"You know. Two men discussing me."

A little angrily, I said, "It wasn't like that."

"He said you brought it up. That you knew about us. It sounded like you used that information to pressure him to tell you stuff."

"Maybe that's how it came up," I said. "I didn't mean anything by it."

"It seemed like you did."

"Doug knows more than he's saying," I said. "I needed to push his buttons a little bit. I never meant to do something that would hurt you."

"Except that you did."

"Did what?"

"Hurt me."

I HUNG UP, FEELING drained and also miffed. I wasn't sure what to make of her call. I hadn't meant to hurt her. Yet part of me saw her point: I'd taken something private and used it as a crowbar on Freeley. And I'd done so knowing full well that, throwing all professional obligations and standards to the wind, I'd developed some feelings for Anne. Had I used her? Did I have any other choice? She must have realized that I couldn't help her and hold what she'd told me in total confidence. Or had she?

I interrupted these ruminations long enough to throw a box of pasta into the boiling water and begin sautéing a pound of the garlic sausage in olive oil. I pulled a Black Label out of the refrigerator and drained half the can. I sat back down at my computer and stared numbly at the screen.

To my surprise, there was a response from the BMV sitting at the bottom of my e-mails, time-marked 5:03 p.m. Somebody had stayed past closing time for me. "Much appreciated," I wrote back. I opened the PDF attachment, saw that it was a result for Beth, then realized to my disappointment they'd turned up hardly anything at all. On top of the two local tickets I'd found, they'd added just one more, out of county, from last year. Then I looked at the form a little more closely. The speeding violation was from Scioto County.

The home of Danny Reilly.

ALL I GOT WHEN I called the number for Portsmouth Municipal Court was a recording, which was par for the course given the time of day. There was no way to leave a message. Not five minutes later, however, I was looking at the details of the ticket on the court's online records website. On August 10 of last year, Beth Freeley had been stopped for doing 75 in a 50 mph zone and ticketed $134. A month later she'd paid the fine by check. The last name of the arresting officer was Maxwell, with the state patrol.

Thank you, Internet, I said, as I looked up the number for the Portsmouth post and dialed.

A female voice answered right away, identifying herself as "Dispatch."

I said, "I'm looking for a Trooper Maxwell."

"Just missed him," she said. "He was working overtime on a car-deer and just wrapped up. Can anyone else help you?"

"Don't think so. Do you know when he'll be back?"

"Tomorrow morning, 7 a.m. May I take a message?"

"Sure," I said.

I obliged her with my name and number and hung up. I stared at the screen. Was I making too much of this? Sure, Danny Reilly was from Portsmouth, and sure, Beth Freeley had reacted funny when I brought up his name. But who cared? Plenty of people drove down to southern Ohio all the time, and none of them had any connection with Reilly. Maybe Beth did makeup house calls down there. Maybe she was visiting relatives. Maybe I'd been on this case too long.

I was rolling this around in my mind and trying to figure out my next move when a more pressing concern brought itself to my attention.

"Shit," I said, jumping up.

I'd burned the sausage.

# 34

I WAS UP AT 6 A.M. THE NEXT DAY, AND THE first thing I thought of, after I realized how much my knee still ached and my head still throbbed, was *Today's the day I get the laptop back.*

I had shaved, had some coffee and was sitting at my dining room table over my third bowl of Cheerios scrolling through an Associated Press preview of the Michigan game on my phone when my reading was interrupted by a call. It was 7:01 a.m.

"This is Billy Maxwell," the voice on the line said. "Did you leave a message? Andy Hayes? Are you the, you know, real Andy Hayes?"

"I suppose it depends on what you mean by real."

"I knew it," he said. "Nobody around here would believe me. Nobody around here knows anything about Ohio State. It's all Bengals down here. Bengals and Reds. So I was really excited when I saw you called."

I wasn't sure what to do with this kind of enthusiasm. It was rare, exceedingly rare, in my experience. So I plowed ahead, told him what I needed.

"Beth Freeley," he said. "Year ago August? I'm going to have to check. Can you give me five minutes?"

"You're the one doing me a favor," I said.

"Call you right back," he said.

And sure enough, five minutes and no more than three spoonfuls of cereal and two more AP stories later, my phone rang again.

"I got it," Maxwell said. "I know exactly who you're talking about it. I mean, normally I wouldn't remember a single driver like that. I write a lot of tickets, if you know what I mean. But—you've met her, right?—she's kind of good looking. At least that's what I thought at first."

"You only thought she was good looking at first?"

"That came out funny, didn't it? What I meant was, I thought she was good looking right away, but after I'd been standing there a minute I realized she looked familiar. Like I'd seen her before. And I told her so. 'Do I happen to know you, ma'am? You look very familiar. Are you from around here?' Like that."

"What'd she say?"

"She was polite. Said I must have been mistaken. Said she was from Columbus."

"Where did you think you knew her from?"

"High school, I figured."

"Where'd you go to school?"

"Portsmouth. Sort of."

"Sort of?"

"Parents got divorced after my sophomore year. Went to live with my mom in Chillicothe and didn't get back very often after that. So I knew a few people in high school real well, but then after I left it was different."

"And she said she hadn't gone to high school with you?"

"Said I had her confused with someone else. She was from Columbus. Said that a couple of times. Frankly, I was inclined to believe her. I'm not great with names and faces generally. There was just something about her."

"Did she say what she was doing down there?"

"Not that I recall. That was U.S. 23, just north of Portsmouth. Busy road. Lot of people. I stop drivers from all over the country there. Had a guy from Alaska two weeks ago. Lot from Columbus. Pretty common."

It was just as I had feared. It still seemed odd that Beth had been in southern Ohio. But so had probably hundreds of other people from Columbus, none of whom knew Danny Reilly.

Just for the heck of it, I asked if Reilly's name rang a bell. Maxwell apologized, said it didn't.

"I appreciate your help," I said. "Anything I might have left out?"

"Don't think so. Hope this helps. Kind of interesting, your line of work."

"Interesting," I agreed. It was rare for a cop to express anything but disdain for what I did. "I'm not sure what this means, or if it's even important. But every little bit counts."

"Let me know if I can do anything else. And let me know if you're ever in the neighborhood. Love to buy you a beer, talk some football."

"I'll keep that in mind," I said, wondering whether it had slipped his mind that I was possibly the most reviled individual in Ohio sports history.

AT EIGHT O'CLOCK I called Brenda Brown. It was obvious I'd awakened her, and she told me to call back in a couple of hours. I was going to argue the point, but she hung up and didn't pick up when I redialed.

I spent the rest of the morning on the usual important private eye duties, which included cleaning up the kitchen from the sausage fiasco the night before, walking the dog, and making a run to the grocery store. My left knee was still stiff and my headache wouldn't go away. At 11 o'clock I bowed to the inevitable and lay down on my couch.

An hour later I awakened to the sound of my cell phone.

"It's Cindy Morris," the voice said.

"What can I do for you?"

"You've been talking to Doug Freeley again."

"And how would you know that? Got another drone following me?"

"We just know," she said.

"You're doing that 'We' thing again."

"Don't push me, Andy. This is getting serious."

"Tell me something I don't know. And thanks a lot for going to see Burke Cunningham, by the way. That was a big help."

"I'm going to see a lot more people if I don't start getting some cooperation. So I'll repeat myself: what were you talking to Freeley about?"

"None of your business," I said. But of course, now that I knew about the files on Anne's laptop, that wasn't quite true.

"It's all our business at this point."

"I'll take your word for it."

"I don't understand why you're being this way."

"What way?"

"So uncooperative. What's so important to take such a risk?"

"A risk like what?"

"The risk of not helping your government."

"I take risks all the time," I said. "For my clients. Not you."

"Doug Freeley's a client now?"

"That would be none of your business either. Except in this case I'll say no, he's not my client."

"Then who is?"

"Back to my original answer. Sorry, but are we finished? I've got things to do."

"Like what?"

"Like things."

"Andy," she said. "Listen carefully. I can't keep your name out of this much longer. We're running out of time."

"I'm aware of that," I said. "Believe me."

I GOT UP AND tried Brenda's phone again. This time she was at the store, she said, but promised to be home shortly. So I made myself lunch and sat down at the computer and tried to do more research. I opened a Word file and reviewed the list of possible suspects. But the names swam before my eyes, and soon I found myself creating a new list, of the people I'd made angry over the past week and a half working on this case. I started with my two ex-wives, then wrote my sons' names, Joe and Mike. Then: Burke, Cindy Morris, Fielding, and, last but not least, Anne Cooper. I reflected that Pastor Roy was about the only person I hadn't offended. Him and Theresa, his latest project from the streets. Except I think she was mad I wouldn't conduct any business with her. So I added her name to the list after all.

Knowing I was wasting time, I tried Brenda's number again. She was back to not answering. I was just thinking I might have to drive to her house when my phone signaled a call from a state office number. A woman from the Department of Administrative Services.

"I've got that file you wanted. Danny Reilly? Sorry it took so long. It was in a warehouse."

"No problem," I said. "Just glad you found it."

"If you'll give me an address I'll stick a copy in the mail."

"Can you fax it? Or PDF it? I'm in a bit of a hurry."

"It's pretty big," she said. "Any chance you could pick it up?"

"On my way," I said.

THE LEGISLATURE WAS IN session, so I had to park in the third and deepest level in the Statehouse parking garage. Nevertheless, I was in the Administrative Services' lobby on the fortieth floor of the Rhodes tower less than twenty minutes after getting the call, and a minute after that a roundish black woman whose badge identified her as "Unit Manager" walked through a pair of glass doors with a manila envelope in her hand. She was wearing an Ohio State sweatshirt and a "Beat Michigan" button and had a string of buckeyes around her neck.

"We got started a little early on the big game," she said with a smile as she handed me the envelope. "Oh my," she said, her smile fading as she recognized me. "I didn't realize." Her hand drifted unconsciously to the button on her sweatshirt.

"Much obliged," I said, and retreated to the elevator.

I had retrieved my Odyssey and was heading back down Third Street toward German Village when Brenda Brown called.

"Finally," I said.

"Been busy." There was a bit of echo on the line; she had the phone on speaker mode.

"I'm ready to do this," I said. "Any time you are."

"I'm going to need a ride," she said slowly. "Could you pick me up?"

"You use up all that gas already?" I said.

"Car trouble," she said after a moment.

"Sure," I said. "I'll be there as soon as I can."

"Mr. Hayes," she said.

"Yes?"

"You'll bring it with you, right?" Her voice sounded stiff.

"What?"

"The laptop. Like we discussed. You'll bring it with you?"

"The laptop," I said.

"That's right."

I didn't say anything for a moment. Kept an eye on the traffic in front of me. Something was wrong here. Her attitude was gone, replaced by something else. Something tense.

Phone on speaker. Asking me to bring the laptop we both knew I didn't have.

"Sure," I said. "I'll bring the laptop. Just like we talked about."

"Thanks," Brenda said, and hung up.

I crossed Livingston and pulled over into a space just past Katzinger's Deli on Third. I unlocked my phone and dialed.

"Andy," Roy said when he answered. "What's happening?"

"You feel like taking a field trip?"

"Now?"

"Now," I said.

THE SHADES WERE DRAWN when I walked up the stairs to Brenda's porch, and only a little light showed at the edges of her windows. I knocked on the door. I looked at the neighboring houses to the left and right. It was nearly dark now and had started to rain.

Darryl Nysong opened the door, a smile like Christmas morning on his face.

"Look who the cat's about to drag in," he said, jabbing the end of my own baseball bat in my chest.

The first thing I noticed when I walked in was the shattered screen of the TV her granddaughter had been watching the last time I was there. These guys must have a thing for smashing glass. Next was the sight of Brenda's meager belongings everywhere, indicative of a good ransacking—it reminded me of the job they did on my place. Then there was Brenda herself, sitting on the couch but slumped a bit to the side, looking like she'd been treated about the same way they'd handled Mary Miller.

"OK, Woody," said Freddie, who was sitting next to Brenda. "Time to wrap things up."

I stood, not moving, surveying the mess.

I said, "How'd you asswipes get here, anyway?"

"Watch your language," Darryl said.

"Answer the question."

"We read the same obituary as you," said Freddie. "We're not stupid."

"That's debatable," I said. "Fletcher know you're here? Breaking the law—again?"

"Shut the fuck up," Darryl said. "Where's the laptop. That's all we want."

"Where's Jayme?" I said to Brenda.

"Upstairs," she said. "TV in the upstairs bedroom."

"There's one thing in your favor," I said to Freddie.

"My favor?" he said.

"You hurt that kid, I would've spilled your guts."

Freddie stood up. "Listen, Hayes," he said. "I can fuck you up now or I can fuck you up later. But either way, I want the laptop. Game's over. Where is it?"

"What if I don't have it?"

"Then you're going to be sorry."

"Sorry about what? You didn't have much luck last time. Couldn't even handle me and a girl."

He took another step forward, and this time there was a knife in his hands.

"Easy now," I said.

"Don't worry," Freddie said. "This isn't for you." He stepped back, walked over to the couch, to Brenda. Pushed her head back as her eyes widened. Held the blade to her throat, but looked at me. "Laptop, dickwad."

After a long moment, during which I swallowed my anger, I said, "It's outside. In my van."

"That's more like it."

"Put the knife down," I said. "She's got nothing to do with any of this."

Instead, Freddie nodded at Darryl.

Darryl smacked the baseball bat in his hand. My baseball bat.

"Let's go," he said.

We walked outside into the dark and the rain. I looked around for Roy, but the sidewalk was empty.

"Where is it?" Darryl said.

"Over there," I said, pointing.

"Move."

I descended the stairs, walked through the yard and its chaos of toys, and opened the gate to the sidewalk. Darryl followed, jabbing my back with the bat. "Come on," he said.

I limped toward my van, trying to figure out my next move, wondering where the heck Roy was, when I heard a woman's voice.

"Hey, you," she said. "Could you give me a ride?"

We both turned and stared. There, just a few feet down the sidewalk, stood Theresa from the soup kitchen, materializing as if from nowhere. I gaped. Maybe it was the rain or the bad light or the adrenaline or what appeared to be the profusion of makeup she'd obviously put on, but she looked half-pretty. Half like someone you'd actually turn your head to look at, briefly, before seeing the face behind the mask.

"What the fuck?" Darryl said, distracted for half a second, but that's all the time I needed. I slammed him sideways, into a van parked on the street. The side of the van, shaded so I hadn't noticed it before, read "Church of the Holy Apostolic Fire." Darryl hit hard and slumped a bit, which was a good thing because the effort had sent white lines of pain up and down my already aching body. He tried to stand, but then stopped, frozen, staring again. But not at Theresa.

"Please don't move," Roy said, holding a gun two feet in front of Darryl's face. "I picked up the jitters in Iraq, and my finger's really twitchy."

We trussed Darryl with some rope that Roy had helpfully brought along and stuffed him into the back of the van, lashing him to the floor with rings meant for moving stuff so he wouldn't roll around too much. Then Roy, Theresa, and I went back through the gate, up the stairs and onto the porch. Theresa knocked loudly. Then a second time. The third time Freddie flung the door open.

"What the hell?" he said when he saw her.

"Gimme five bucks and I'll suck your cock," she said in that sweet, nicotine-coated voice I'd come to know so well.

He stared in disbelief, then poked his head out the door a little farther. "Darryl?"

"He's tied up," I said, as Roy raised his gun.

FREDDIE NEEDED MORE PERSUADING than Darryl to get into the van, but Roy was nothing if not good at winning arguments. He was a pastor, after all.

"You need help with them?"

"Don't worry," Roy said. "I've got it all worked out."

"Nothing rough, OK? I don't want to make this any worse than it already is."

"I've got you covered," Roy said.

"You sure you don't need a hand?"

"Best not," he said. "Too many cooks."

"Or witnesses."

"Whatever."

"By the way," I said. "Theresa? That was my back-up? Seriously?"

He looked across the seat at her. She was staring at me.

"She wanted to help. And I've been trying to get her to take more responsibility for herself."

"I guess," I said. I looked at her. "Thanks. I still owe you breakfast."

"Suck your cock for five bucks," she said.

I looked at Roy.

"Baby steps," he said.

After Roy had pulled away, Brenda and I put Jayme's car seat into my van, and then the three of us drove downtown to the jail. Brenda unloaded on me on the way, complaining about the mess they'd made of her house and the loss of her TV and Freddie's body odor and several other matters that were all thanks to me and that she was perfectly right to be upset about. At the jail, while I waited for Barry and her to deal with the paperwork on her son, I called Joseppi's Pizza on Sullivant and ordered two large pizzas. Half an hour later, Dave out of jail and sitting in the back of the van playing with Jayme, we picked up the pizzas, then drove back to Brenda's.

"How about it," I said to Brenda as I parked.

"How about what?"

"The laptop. Remember our deal?"

"Our deal didn't include those fuckheads wrecking my house and holding me hostage."

"I'm sorry about that," I said. "I'm going to make it right by you. But first I need my laptop."

From the back, Dave said, "What are you talking about?"

"Shut up," Brenda said. "Don't listen to him."

"The laptop Mary Miller gave your mom. It's mine. I need it back. Your mom said she'd ask you where it was if I got you out of jail."

"Shit," he said. He was thin, with a buzz haircut and a dragon tattoo on the back of his neck. "I could have told you that any time. Thing's a piece of shit. Hardly any memory."

"Shut up, Dave," Brenda said.

"It's upstairs, in my room. Propping up the TV. Only way it got decent reception."

"Damn it, Dave," Brenda said.

While he was inside retrieving it, I said to Brenda, "Keep the rest of the bond money, once Barry's taken his cut. Least I can do." I swallowed hard as I said it, remembering how tough it had been to come up with that amount.

She stared at me. "You are one piece of work, Hayes. You know that?"

"It's been suggested to me, yes."

Dave came outside, through the yard and up to the van. He handed me the computer. I checked the sticker. It was the one.

"Piece of shit," he said. "No idea why you'd want it."

"That makes two of us," I said.

# 35

THE FIRST THING I DID WHEN I GOT HOME
was turn up the heat and throw the rest of last night's pasta in
the stove. Then I grabbed a Black Label from the refrigerator,
reconsidered, and rewarded myself with a Columbus Brewing
Company bottle instead. I went into the bathroom, undressed,
and stood in the shower until the hot water began to run out.
Throwing on sweats and the thickest bathrobe I had, I wolfed
down dinner while I channel-surfed the cable stations. Finally,
about an hour later, I was recovered enough to get back to work.

After all I'd been through, you'd think I would have been
more excited to hold the laptop again, but there was a feeling
of letdown as I typed in the password, brought the computer
menu up, and started deleting Pete Freeley's offending video
files. I just wanted to get it over with. I briefly considered deleting Doug's business files as well, those incriminating spreadsheets that the FBI would no doubt love to get their hands on,
but thought better of it. As troublesome as they were, those
items weren't part of my case. Better to let this sleeping dog
lie, I thought.

At nine o'clock I texted Anne. "Give me a call," I wrote. It was all I could think to say. I tried again ten minutes later, same message, and a minute later the phone rang.

"Andy," she said.

"I'm sorry to bother you so late," I said.

"It's all right," she said. "I just saw your message. Listen, I'm sorry about what I said. Earlier."

"It's OK," I said, and told her why I was calling.

TWENTY MINUTES LATER, CHANGED back into street clothes, I was sitting in the driveway of her parents' house in the Indian Trails subdivision in Grove City. She was beside me in the passenger seat of the van, holding the laptop.

"Thank you," she said again.

"You're welcome," I said, also again.

"The files?"

"Your papers are still on there. That's up to you. All of Pete's videos are off, but that's part of my arrangement with my original client. Also . . ."

"Yes?"

"You might consider changing the password."

She half smiled. She said, "What about Darryl and Freddie?"

"I don't think they're going to be bothering anyone anymore."

Her eyes widened. I said, "Nothing like that. My friend and I had some friendly words with them. It should be all worked out."

"Fletcher?"

"If you're asking me, I'd advise you to quit that job for good."

"That won't be a problem," she said. "I never want to see him again."

"At the same time . . ."

"Yes?"

"There's the possibility he could still make trouble for you."

"That's what I'm afraid of."

"Me too."

"Is there anything I can do about that?"

"I'm not sure. I'm weighing our options in that department."

"Our options?"

"Something like that," I said hurriedly. "Give me a little time."

"All I've got right now," she said.

After a silence bordering on the uncomfortable, I said, "Any further word from Doug?"

After an equally uncomfortable pause, she said, "He wants to see me again. Talk about us. About our future."

"Your future?"

"That's right."

"How do you feel about that?"

"I don't know," she said.

"After everything he did—" I started, but she stopped me, holding up her hand.

"Don't," she said. She opened the door and had started to climb out of the Odyssey when she stopped and turned.

"One more question?"

"Fire away."

"I've never understood why your nickname is Woody."

"Was Woody."

"Was, right."

"He's the most famous football coach in Ohio State history, maybe in the country. I played football pretty well for a time."

"But you're not a coach. Was it just the football connection?"

I hesitated. "You know how his career ended?"

"Everyone knows that. He punched the Clemson player at the '78 Gator Bowl."

"Very good," I said.

"Big Buckeye family, remember?"

I said, "When I was a freshman in high school, we were in a state playoff game up in Canton."

"OK."

"We only had a couple of black kids on our team that year. One was a guy named Marcus Jedder. I was quarterbacking that night and Marcus was running back."

"You were quarterback? As a freshman?"

"Like I said, it's all on Wikipedia. Anyway, Marcus was having the game of his life. He was keeping us competitive with this team from southern Ohio that should have been killing us."

"Sounds exciting."

"It was," I said. "But the other team was riding Marcus the whole time. Racist stuff, names, slurs, every time we lined up. Constant, trying to get under his skin."

"That's awful."

I realized I hadn't told this story in a while. For good reason. I said, "Minute to go, I pull a fake, hand to Marcus and he takes off downfield. Winning touchdown."

"Good for him."

"Damn straight. But then this big lineman from the other team makes a crack. A bad one."

"What'd he say?"

I hesitated again.

"It's OK," she said. "I'm a big girl."

"He said, 'Somebody send that fucking coon back to the jungle.' "

"That's terrible."

"Said it loudly too, so he knew we could hear him. It was meant for us."

"So what'd you do?"

I paused. "I punched him."

"You *punched* him?"

"Yes I did."

"You punched him. Right on the field."

"Almost exactly the fifty-yard line."

"What happened?"

"Well, he went down. Hard. Then—there was a bit of a melee."

"A melee."

"Or perhaps more of an old-fashioned rumble. You probably get the picture."

"So what did they do to you?"

"To me? Nothing. All the coaches and everybody in the stands were looking at Marcus downfield so nobody saw it except the players, and they weren't talking. Plus, no smart phones in those days so there were no pictures or video."

"You punched him," Anne said. "So you became 'Woody' Hayes."

"My teammates started it. And then it spread. The nickname," I added. "Not that story."

"What happened to Marcus?"

"He's a surgeon now, over at Ohio State."

"Amazing."

"And the really amazing thing? That same lineman, the one I punched? A few years ago he was in a car accident and they brought him into the emergency room, and he looks up and who's the doctor who's going to save his life? Marcus Jedder."

"You're kidding."

I smiled. "Actually, yes," I said. "About the accident. But not about Marcus being a doctor or about my nickname. But wouldn't that make a great story?"

She didn't respond right away. Instead, she looked out the windshield at her parents' garage. Then she looked back, a half smile on her face.

"Always the joker," she said, a little sadly.

And that was that. She didn't invite me in, and I didn't suggest we go anywhere.

"Thanks again," she said, as she got out of the Odyssey.

"Good night," I said.

ROY CALLED JUST AS I was exiting onto Greenlawn Avenue off of I-71.

"All set," he said.

"I'm afraid to ask."

"You know where West Jefferson is?"

"Village—way out west on U.S. 40?"

"That's the place. We took them ten miles past that. Tossed them out and made them strip. Everything off."

"Jesus, Roy," I said. "It's thirty degrees out and raining. You ever heard of hypothermia?"

"Relax," he said. "Like I said, I've got it covered."

"Covered."

"You remember those Michigan jackets? From the drop-off box?"

"You didn't."

"Fitted them real nice. Turns out I also had some Michigan sweats and sweatshirts and gloves and hats I hadn't itemized yet. Must have been a real joker, whoever dropped all that off."

"You dressed Freddie and Darryl in Michigan stuff."

"Head to toe," Roy said. "Threw in some long underwear and extra socks to boot. Toasty warm."

"Then what?"

"I gave them each a flashlight and an umbrella and a bottle of water and told them to walk home. Slowly."

"What'd they say?"

"Not much. They pretty much stopped talking once I gave them the jackets."

"How far out are they?"

"Twenty, thirty miles. I lost track. Take them all night, that's for sure."

"Probably use the exercise."

"My thought exactly."

# 36

I WAS SO TIRED BY THE TIME I GOT HOME I only had enough strength to push Hopalong into the backyard, stand for the minute it took him to do his business, then collapse into bed and fall asleep almost immediately.

I was awakened the next morning by the throbbing in my head. After stumbling downstairs for more pain relievers and coffee, I grabbed Reilly's personnel file, sat down on the couch, coffee in hand, and started to read. It was all pretty simple. Reilly had gone to work at the Portsmouth State Youth Detention Center at age twenty, his sole experience with kids up to that point consisting, apparently, of driving an ice cream truck one summer. His five-page application made up most of the file, followed by several letters and forms from the agency laying out the terms of his employment after he was hired. The final three pages consisted of a letter informing Reilly he was suspended for violations of two administrative rules of conduct, a letter from a union representative informing the state that the union would not be contesting the disciplinary process on behalf of Mr. Reilly, and a letter of dismissal dated twenty-four years ago. The explanation for his firing seemed consistent with the Reilly I knew and loved: smuggling contraband into the facility in the form of marijuana, and "consorting with an adjudicated youth for the intent purpose of committing an illegal act."

Fascinating, I thought. But what exactly did it mean?

After another cup of coffee I took Hopalong to the park, feeling guilty about the uneven exercise schedule he'd been on since Ted Hamilton walked into my life almost two weeks ago. That reminded me I owed him a call to say I'd found the laptop and everything was, once again, over and done with. But I couldn't bring myself to do it. I kept thinking about Emily Goodwin and the Grandview Yard quarry.

Once I got back I started to make a mental list of the things I had to do, from contacting Special Agent Morris to see if I could get her off my back now that I officially didn't have the laptop anymore, to seeing if I could make things right with Fielding. As I sat on the couch I realized my decision making might benefit from shutting my eyes for a minute. When I opened them again, the clock read 11:30. I'd been out for two hours. I was due in Bexley in half an hour. Of all the places I wanted to be right then.

With an extra effort I managed to pull onto the Huntingtons' street and into my usual surveillance spot three doors down right at noon. And waited. And waited. At 12:30 Honey's red BMW was still sitting in the driveway. Something was amiss. I thought about bagging the job and going home, but that ran the risk she was just running late and I'd miss her and the money shot. Then there was that nagging feeling about the case I couldn't shake. If I bailed now, would I ever figure out what was bothering me?

Finally, because I couldn't think of anything else to do, I looked up the number for Banninger's Buttons and called the store.

"I'm sorry to bother you," I told the young-sounding

woman who answered the phone. "This is such an odd request. But I'm trying to find a friend of mine. Honey Huntington? I know she comes by the store sometimes and I needed to leave her a message."

"Oh sure, Honey," the woman said. "She's so great. But she's not here."

"Any idea when she might be coming by?"

"I don't think she's coming today. I heard Helen say she was sick."

"Helen?"

"Ms. Banninger. You know, the owner."

"Of course. Well that's too bad."

"I know. I just love them. They're such a great couple."

"Aren't they?" I said.

"Can I leave Honey a message?"

"I don't think so, thanks. I'll try another time."

IT TOOK ME NO more than ten minutes to get from Honey's house to the administrative building at McCulloh College. Might as well get it over with, I reasoned. I had just pulled in when who should I see pulling out in a new-looking Volvo but Henry Huntington himself. I waved in his direction, but he didn't see me, distracted, talking on his cell phone, *tsk tsk,* and exited the lot rather quickly. Curious, I executed a K turn in the parking lot and followed him as discreetly as possible down first one leafy college street, then another. Suddenly he turned down an alley. I hesitated for just a moment and then, curiosity heightened, followed as far back as I could. He crossed an intersecting alley, put his brakes on, then pulled into a garage behind a yellow clapboard house. The garage door was closing as I drove past, turned right at the next intersection, and reemerged on Bennett Street. I circled the block and pulled the Odyssey up in front of the yellow house a minute later.

Not knowing what else to do, I climbed the stairs and

knocked on the door. I waited my customary minute, then knocked again. Normally, I start writing out a note after the second knock goes unanswered. Not this time.

It was almost time for the fourth knock when I heard a latch click. The door opened and a woman, her glasses askew, peered through the screen. Late twenties or early thirties, pretty, pushing back curly brown hair that looked, there was no other way to put it, a tad disheveled.

"Yes?" she said.

"Sorry to trouble you," I lied. "I'm looking for Henry Huntington."

The expression on her face told me I'd come to the right place, although she still tried a halfhearted, "You must have the wrong address."

"Probably not," I said. Some gears were finally starting to click, and I knew my patience was limited. "I need to talk to him. It's important. I'll wait out here."

"Like I said, you have the wrong address."

"It's OK. I saw him pull into your garage. Just tell him it's about his wife."

Huntington was at the door less than two minutes later, and it would be an understatement to say he did not look pleased. Although he did, in point of fact, also look a bit disheveled.

"Hayes," he said. "This had better be good."

"It's not," I said. "It's bad."

"What are you talking about?"

"You've made me realize what an incompetent investigator I am. Like I needed any more reminding."

"I don't understand."

"You hired me to find out if Honey was having an affair between the hours of noon and 2 p.m. It never occurred to me you might have another reason for wanting to know what she was doing at that time."

"This is ridiculous."

"If you were assured she was occupied, it meant you were safe on your own appointed rounds."

"You're out of your mind."

"You wanted to make sure *she* wasn't following *you*. Isn't that right?"

"Don't be foolish," Huntington said. "I'm here on college business."

"You missed a button," I said.

"What?"

"The top of your shirt," I said. "It's misbuttoned."

Huntington reddened and quickly addressed the sartorial mishap, just as the object of his attention reappeared in the doorway, looking a little less disheveled and a lot more angry.

"I'm going to insist that you leave," she said. "You have no right to be here."

Without replying, I reached for my cell phone, brought it up with just enough speed and finesse to justify the inordinate amount of time I'd spent practicing this, and snapped a quick picture of the pair.

"I was just going," I said.

What do you know. I got the money shot after all.

I WAS HALFWAY HOME, still fuming over my stupidity, when something occurred to me. A way to make up for ignoring my gut for so long with Henry and Honey. I pulled into Wolfe Park on the western edge of Bexley, parked by the tennis courts, and dialed the Portsmouth post of the Ohio State Highway Patrol. Maxwell wasn't there. But he called back in five minutes.

"Andy," he said. "What's going on?"

"Listen, Billy," I said. "You remember Beth Freeley? How you were certain you'd seen her before?"

"Sure. Been thinking about it ever since you called."

"Is there anywhere else you can check to see if you might be right? Anybody who might know her?"

"I'm sure there is. Let me think about it, OK?"

"Anything you can do," I said. "It's important to trust your gut."

"Ain't that the truth," he said.

I WAS JUST ABOUT to pull back onto Broad Street when my phone buzzed. A text from Anne.

*It's all good with Doug. We worked everything out. Seeing him this afternoon. Tx.*

Worked everything out. What was that supposed to mean?

*Where?* I texted in return.

I waited, but no answer. I put the phone on the passenger seat and drove home. I was pulling into a free spot on Lansing, keeping one eye out for wild-eyed guys with shotguns, when I got her follow-up text.

*The cabin. Hocking Hills.*

That's great, I thought. That is truly great. She gets the laptop and her guy, I get—what?

Back home, I pulled my running clothes on and grabbed Hopalong's leash. At times like this, the best I could do was drown my sorrows in a workout. The fact I was still barely able to walk, let alone jog, was beside the point.

Normally I can circle the park in nine minutes, eight and a half if I'm feeling peppy. We averaged sixteen minutes a lap today. Stubbornly, in more pain than I cared to admit, we went three times. I was miserable; Hopalong was in heaven. But at least I'd worked up a sweat that didn't involve someone hitting me.

I was stretching in the living room when Billy Maxwell called again.

"Man, you're not going to believe this," he said.

"Try me."

"I thought about what you said. About my gut. And I started thinking about it. Called my wife, asked her what she thought. She suggested I look her up in a yearbook. Smart, you know? Guess that's why I call her my better half. So I just drove over to the high school."

"Good idea."

"So, small world, turns out I went to school with the gal who's the librarian. She gets out my sophomore yearbook, and I'm looking through it, and sure enough, there's no Beth Freeley."

"Shit," I interrupted. "I found something that said her maiden name might be Jones. Forgot to tell you."

"Well, that's what Patty Lou said. The librarian. Maybe she'd gotten married and changed her name. Duh. So on a lark we decided to flip to the end of the pictures and just work our way forward."

"And?"

"So, darned if she wasn't like three pictures from the back of the tenth graders. I was right after all."

"What?"

"Beth Freeley. There she was. I would have recognized her anywhere. We were in English class together. No question about it. I think I had a little crush on her. Maybe that's why her face struck me the day I stopped her. Yeah, twenty years younger, but it was her. Even with the hair."

"The hair?"

"She's a blonde now. But she was dark back then. Maybe that's what threw me off the day I stopped her. Changing your hair can do funny things like that. My wife had some highlights put in one day without telling me, and I almost didn't recognize her when she dropped by the post afterward."

"How about that," I said, patiently.

"But here's the thing. It wasn't just her last name that had changed. Her whole name was different. It wasn't Beth at all. It was Lisa. And her last name wasn't Jones. Her name was Lisa B. Wheeler. Maybe the B's for Beth, I don't know. But it was her, no question."

For the first time in our conversation I started paying close attention. Could this be right? Had Maxwell really found Beth Freeley? The real Beth Freeley?

"I'm listening," I said.

"Good, because that's only half of it," Maxwell said.

"What do you mean?"

"Well, after I was done looking at this picture, I turned to Patty Lou. She's got this real funny look on her face. I asked her what was wrong."

"What'd she say?"

"She looked at me, and then looked at the picture, and said, 'This lady you gave the traffic ticket to. It was her? This girl?' I told her I was sure. She said it was impossible, that it couldn't be. Want to guess why?"

I had a sinking feeling in my stomach. "The girl in the picture was dead?"

"You're absolutely right."

"I am?"

"I mean, you're absolutely right—that's what I thought she was going to say too. But that's not it at all."

"What is it then?"

"The girl in the picture, Lisa Wheeler, was arrested two months into her senior year."

"Arrested? For what?"

"For killing her father. Blew a hole in his chest with a shotgun."

# 37

AFTER I HUNG UP I REALIZED I WAS trembling. This couldn't be right. Beth, the makeup home saleswoman, the New Albany matron, a killer?

I logged onto my computer and went to the *Dispatch* archives. This time it didn't take any time at all to find what I was looking for.

"*Portsmouth Girl Held In Father's Fatal Shooting.*"

"*Portsmouth Teen Could Be Tried As Adult In Dad's Death.*"

"*Judge Denies Bail For Portsmouth Teen In Dad's Killing.*"

"*Portsmouth Girl To Be Tried In Juvenile Court.*"

"*Portsmouth Teen Delinquent In Dad's Death.*"

"*Portsmouth Girl Who Killed Dad Sentenced To Detention Center.*"

I read the articles with a growing sense of disbelief. There was only one thing missing to fill out the picture, and that was literally a picture. The paper's archived stories were text only.

Despite the aches and pains from my ill-advised jog, I was out the door ten minutes later. Five minutes after that I was in the underground parking garage at the Main Library at Grant and State Streets. And five minutes after that I was sitting down at a microfilm machine while a library staffer was politely explaining how to work the knobs and handles.

I only needed to look at the very first story.

It was just like Maxwell had said. The girl in the picture, the girl sitting at a table in a jail uniform, was a brunette. And young. So terribly young. But there was no question about it. The defendant named Lisa B. Wheeler was the woman I knew as Beth Freeley.

I walked back to my car in a daze, so deep in thought that I forgot to have my parking ticket punched and had to walk back upstairs to the machine in the lobby. I finally pulled out of the garage and turned right and then right again, and then pulled over next to the Topiary Park and its bushes sculpted in the manner of Seurat's *Sunday Afternoon on the Isle of La Grande Jatte*. I stared at them, but I wasn't seeing. I had just thought of something else.

I was home again in less than ten minutes. I pulled up the last story in the *Dispatch* archives, then flipped through Reilly's personnel file.

Shit, I said to myself. Shit.

The dates matched up perfectly. Lisa B. Wheeler, aka Beth Freeley, had been at the Portsmouth State Youth Detention Facility, more than two decades ago, at almost exactly the same time Danny Reilly had been a guard there.

**THERE WAS SO MUCH** to do that I didn't know where to start. Should I get ahold of Doug Freeley, or Fielding? Drive immediately to New Albany to see if Beth was home? Let Special Agent Morris know her case had probably just gotten a lot more complicated? And what about Anne? Did I owe it to her to explain that her lover was married to a possible double killer?

Because who had a better motive for shooting Reilly than the woman whose secret life he was in danger of exposing?

I chose Door Number 1, the Columbus Police Department, and was headed up High Street in that direction when Kevin Harding called from the *Dispatch*.

"Anything new?" he said.

"Not a thing," I said guiltily. "You?"

"Plenty," he said. "Doug Freeley wants to talk to me. I think he wants to get ahead of the story. Anything I should know before we sit down?"

"Congrats," I said. "That's a big get."

"Thanks. So how about it? Anything new?"

"Nothing. When are you meeting him?"

"Couple hours."

I paused. "Couple hours? From now?"

"That's right."

"Where?"

"Max and Erma's, up in Dublin. Right next to his office. Sure you don't have anything?"

"You're meeting Doug Freeley in a couple hours in Dublin."

*It's all good with Doug.*

I looked at my watch. It was almost three-thirty.

"That's right. Want to come along? Make for great copy."

"No thanks," I said.

After we'd hung up I pulled into a parking space opposite the Grange Insurance building. I dialed Freeley's number. No answer. I tried his house, same luck. I used the phone to Google American Financial Health Care. To my surprise, he answered after two rings.

"What the hell do you want?" he said.

"Are you meeting Kevin Harding in Dublin in two hours?"

"That's none of your—"

"Yes or no?"

It might have been the tone of my voice, but after a moment he said, "That's right. So what?"

"I just got a text from Anne Cooper. She said she's meeting you at your cabin in the Hocking Hills. This afternoon."

"What?"

"That's right. Did you say you'd meet her there?"

"No. Are you kidding?"

I thought for a minute. "Did she tell you she got the laptop back?"

"She did?"

"She didn't tell you?"

"No. I haven't been in touch with her in a couple days."

"You haven't communicated with her?"

"No, I swear."

"She says you did. Texted her."

"Impossible."

"Why?"

"I lost my fucking cell phone, that's why, all right? I haven't had it in two days. So how in the hell could I text her?"

*We worked everything out. Seeing him this afternoon.*

"Don't do anything," I said. "Don't move. Don't budge from your phone."

"Why—"

But I'd cut him off. I called Anne. After three rings she picked up.

"Andy?" Her voice was faint, with lots of background noise.

"Anne," I said. "Where are you?"

A short pause. Then: "On my way to the cabin. Like I told you."

"Did you talk to Doug about this?"

"Yes. I told you. We worked everything out."

"No," I said. "Did you talk to him? Talk, not text."

"No," she said. "We texted. We always do. Did."

"He texted you from his phone?"

"That's right."

"When?"

"Just a couple hours ago. Why? What's wrong?"

A thought crossed my mind. "Where's Amelia?"

"With my parents," she said.

I could hardly hear her reply for the background noise. And I could tell the reception was cutting in and out. It was southern Ohio. Notorious for dropped calls.

"Anne," I said. "What did Doug tell you? Text you, I mean."

"We're going to work it out, like I told you. He said to bring the laptop and we'd talk and everything would be fine."

"He told you to bring the laptop?"

But there was no answer. She was gone. I called back, got voicemail. Tried again, and again. Nothing.

I called Doug back.

He said, "Do you mind telling me what the hell is going on?"

"Anne's on the way to your cabin," I said.

"The cabin? Why would Anne go to the cabin?"

"Because your wife told her to," I said.

# 38

I DROVE AS QUICKLY AS I COULD CONSIDERING I was in the company of hundreds of commuters also headed southeast on Route 33 away from Columbus. During the maddening moments when traffic slowed to a stop I called Anne's phone, to no avail. To avoid going crazy I called Billy Maxwell back and asked him to check on one more thing that had occurred to me. He said he didn't mind at all. In the meantime, my phone kept going off with people I didn't want to talk to—Kevin Harding, Ted Hamilton, Henry Fielding—even Burke. I didn't bother answering. I was past the two-minute warning now. Nothing else mattered.

I'd scribbled directions from Freeley on an envelope I'd salvaged from my coat pocket, and those miraculously got me to a dirt road and the cabin after the GPS stopped working for the same reason I hadn't been able to reach Anne. I thought about doing something fancy like turning off my lights, putting the Odyssey in neutral, and gliding quietly up to the house. Instead I gunned it up the gravel drive and lay on the horn.

There were two cars parked in front of the cabin as I skidded to a stop. One was a white Escalade, which I took to be Beth's. Next to it an older-model Honda Civic with a Gore-Lieberman sticker on the bumper, which I knew was Anne's. As I jumped out and limped toward the cabin I wondered briefly what Anne had thought when she'd seen the Escalade, and if it had registered that it was not Doug's car. I got to the door and tried the handle, but it was locked, as I'd expected. I started pounding with my fist. I heard a woman's voice inside, and waited a split second to see if someone would open the door before deciding just to break in instead. Smashing down doors is not as easy as it looks on TV. But it's not all that hard for a guy my size tackling a door on a newer-model vacation cabin that's designed mainly to keep raccoons out.

I stumbled inside and found myself staring across a small living room at Beth Freeley, who was staring back at me with a look someplace between shock and fury, a look enhanced by the gun she was pointing in my direction. To my left, Anne sat in a recliner, her hands and feet tied with clothesline and her mouth bound with duct tape. Her eyes were wide and swollen, and her right cheek, the one without the scar, looked red and puffy, as if she'd just been struck there, and not softly either.

"Put the gun down," I said, breathing hard. "It's over."

The cabin was exposed wood throughout with soft lighting and calico curtains. A half loft overlooked the main living area. Very cozy.

I spied the laptop sitting on the breakfast counter separating the small kitchen from the living room.

"The computer," I said. "Having trouble logging on?"

Beth said, "Not for much longer. Anne was just about to tell me the password."

I said, "I bet she was. Let me repeat: put down the gun."

Wordlessly, Beth shook her head.

"One murder's not enough?" I said. "Or two, if you count your father?"

She stared at me. "You son of a bitch."

"I've been called worse."

"If you know about my father, then you know nothing matters anymore."

"So you're going to kill two more people? Like that's going to help?"

"I will if I have to."

"You're not being logical," I said. "Shooting us isn't going to fix anything. And that's not why you're down here to begin with. Is it?"

I saw a look of doubt creep over her face. It would be nice to know what might have happened next. But instead of some kind of peaceful resolution, all I got was the sound of a car going too fast on a gravel road, a flash of headlights in the house through the open door, a dinging sound as a car door opened and then the slam of the door shutting.

"What the hell?" Doug said as he burst inside. "Beth? What's going on?"

"It's a good question," I said.

"Shut up," Beth said.

"I got here as quickly as I could," Doug said to no one in particular.

"I need the files on the computer," Beth said. "That's all. Doug's files. *Your* files"—glaring at her husband. "That'll fix everything. That's all I want."

"Doug didn't lose his phone, did he?" I said. "Here's my guess. You came across it, realized he and Anne had been texting again, saw she had the laptop back. Perfect chance to solve all your problems at once. Take care of Anne, take care of the files. You're the one who texted her, suggested she come down here. Bring the laptop. Work everything out."

"Beth?" Doug said weakly. "Is that true?"

"Shut up," she said again. "Just shut up."

"Come on, Beth," I said. "It's time."

"I did this for you," Beth said, looking at her husband. "Even after everything you've done, I just did it for you."

I saw Anne's eyes stray for a moment toward Doug, then move back to Beth.

"You made a mistake," Beth said, her voice a little softer. "We all do, God knows. And I forgive you. I really do. I just wanted to fix things. I just wanted to help you."

"Help me," Doug said.

"I was just trying to get these files back. So you'd be all right. So the company would be all right. I just wanted her to give me the password."

"I'm sorry," Doug said. "I'm so sorry."

I said, "Don't listen to her."

Doug turned to me, crestfallen. "What?"

"She's lying to you. Don't listen to her."

"I am not lying," Beth said slowly, anger seeping into her voice.

"Sure you are," I said. "You've been lying from the very beginning. From the moment I walked into your living room."

Doug said, "What are you talking about?"

"Let's start with the basics," I said. "Beth here is not really Beth. Are you? It's Lisa, if memory serves. Which it doesn't. But yearbooks do. Lisa B. Wheeler."

"Yearbooks?" Doug said.

"Let me ask you this," I said to Doug. "Did you never wonder about Beth's family? Ever think it strange you'd never met them?"

"I told you—her parents died in a car accident," he said. "She was raised by her grandparents."

"And where was that?"

A look of confusion crossed his face. "Columbus."

"Ever meet them?"

He shook his head. "No—they were dead too. They were elderly."

"Not that elderly," I said. "Would it surprise you they're still alive?"

"What?"

"And that Beth visits them from time to time? On their farm in Scioto County." Maxwell had dug up that tidbit for me and called me back in time—the last call I got before cell service disappeared.

"She was down there a year ago in August, I'm guessing, though maybe more recently as well."

"Shut up," Beth said. "It's not true. Don't listen to him."

"You shut up," I said.

As succinctly as I could, given the tension in the cabin and the gun in Beth's hand, I explained what I'd found in the old articles about Lisa B. Wheeler. Her father, a violent alcoholic. Years of abuse. Her mother repeatedly battered. Lisa, troubled in school. Her only respite summers with her grandparents. Where she'd learned to shoot.

A particularly bad night. Her mother, already recovering from a beating two nights earlier. Her father, at the door of their trailer, drunk and angry. Lisa, retrieving the shotgun she'd hidden under her bed.

No more beatings for her mother.

It had all come out at trial.

Beth started to cry.

I said, "You met Danny Reilly in juvenile detention when he was a guard. Just long enough to remember you. Who wouldn't remember a girl who killed her own father?"

"That's enough," Doug said, uncertainly. "You don't know what you're saying."

"You got out, came to Columbus. What's that saying in southern Ohio? The importance of the three Rs—Reading, 'Riting, and Route 23 to Columbus? Then you changed your name. Beth Jones. Plain as can be. Became a secretary. Met Doug. Saw your way up. And out. Getting pregnant with Pete just sealed the deal."

"Don't be ridiculous," Doug said.

"And then, the cruelest irony of all. Reilly ends up on a work crew next door to your house in New Albany."

"The mail," Beth said softly.

"What?" Doug said.

"I'd come out to get the mail. Saw Danielle Hastings. Long enough to chat. Long enough for Danny to recognize me. Came over as soon as he had the chance."

"No," Doug said. "That can't be."

I said, "He blackmailed you."

"Not in so many words," Beth said. "He didn't say anything that first day. But he came back, next day, said he was a little short on his rent payment, wondered if I could help him out."

Doug made a sound somewhere between a sigh and a gasp.

"After that, it just took on a life of its own. I gave him five hundred dollars a week and he more or less left me alone. But he wasn't going to let go. One time I missed the payment by a day or two and he came right over. I saw him sitting in his truck across the street. Didn't call, didn't knock on the door. Just sat there."

She said, "I have no idea how long this would have gone on. I kept trying to think of ways to end it. Then the whole thing happened with the laptop, and the company's records, and"—she looked at Anne—"*her*, and I finally saw this opportunity. This window."

"No," Doug said.

"Shut up," she said, wiping away tears with her free hand. "This is all your fault. All of it. We wouldn't be in this mess if it wasn't for you screwing up."

I said, "It was you who sent Danny after me."

"After the laptop," she corrected. "That's all I wanted. The files."

"He got the laptop," I said. "But he didn't give it to you."

"He wanted more money, more than I'd promised him. And . . ."

We waited.

"He said he'd take the payment in kind if I didn't have the cash."

"So you shot him."

"I figured I'd get the laptop some other way. But I'd worked too hard to get where I was to let a loser like Danny Reilly take it away from me."

"If the files fell into the wrong hands, like the police, for example, it could ruin your husband's company."

"Yes," she said, a little stiffly.

"And if the company's ruined, you're not living in New Albany anymore."

She said nothing.

"So retrieving the files was really more about you than your husband," I offered.

"No," she said.

"Grandview Yard quarry," I said.

"What about it?"

I thought back to the residential search I'd run on Doug and Beth on Nexis. How Doug's history had stretched all the way back to Cleveland. How Beth's had started abruptly, in Columbus, at Lakeside Apartments. I hadn't put it together until now. Quarry. Lakeside.

"You had Danny meet you at the quarry because you knew how isolated it was. Because you'd lived there. You'd seen the kids diving. You knew sometimes they didn't come back up."

"Something like that," she said.

"Kill two birds with one stone," I said. "Danny gets you the laptop, then gets what he has coming to him. The fact he didn't deliver the goods made it all the easier." Not to mention the sex extortion he'd implied, I thought.

Silence crept over the room. I could hear the hum of the refrigerator. It was a little chilly, and I realized the door to the cabin was still open.

"One more time," I said. "Time to put the gun down."

"No," Beth said. But something in her voice had changed. She had done the math. It wasn't just that she'd realized killing the three of us was a long shot. It was the fact that no matter what she did, kill us or let us live, it indeed was over. The running. The hiding behind the mansion in New Albany. The pretending she hadn't grown up in a southern Ohio trailer where you prayed on Saturday night that the beatings wouldn't last too long.

"Beth," I said, and took one cautious step forward.

"Don't move," she said sharply. But the gun wasn't aimed at me anymore.

"No," Doug said, realizing a moment later what was happening.

"Beth," I repeated.

"This is all your fault," she said. "All I wanted was the laptop."

At the word "laptop," Beth raised the gun, moving it away from us and toward her mouth. I stood frozen, just for a second, and that would have been just long enough to let Beth carry out her plan had a strange sound not suddenly broken the silence. It was so loud and distinct but also so unfamiliar that we all looked, even Beth, and that fraction of a second of distraction was just enough to snap me out of my immobility. I lunged forward, realizing as I did that the sound was coming from Anne, who was screaming through the tape. Screaming and screaming and screaming. There was another scream, not Anne this time, and a shout, and furniture crashing, and then a louder crash, a gun going off, and then we were all in a pile on the floor by the fireplace, and it was indeed all over. Except that, for better or worse, it was just beginning. For all of us. But especially Beth.

# 39

I USED THE CABIN'S LANDLINE PHONE TO call 911 while Doug and Anne saw to Beth's head wound. When I was done I walked to the couch and looked down at Beth, and without hesitation she looked up and met my gaze. I held it for a moment, then turned around. I walked over to the coffee table, picked up the laptop, and without speaking walked outside. The air was cold, and through the treetops the clear sky above was filled with stars. I walked to my van, opened the back, and set the laptop inside. I thought: all this pain for a machine.

It took almost twenty minutes for the first sheriff's car to arrive, but soon enough the drive was filled with an impressive array of emergency vehicles. Rotating red-and-blue lights lit up the woods. I saw people emerge from the two other cabins in sight of the Freeleys' place and stare in our direction. I waved, but they didn't wave back.

Two young paramedics, a man and a woman, worked on Beth for several minutes as she rocked back and forth on the couch. She kept quiet even when they opened the wound enough to apply some kind of antiseptic. I could tell it was a superficial injury, and I knew she'd been lucky: the bullet had likely glanced off her temple. There was no question, ironically, that Anne had saved her life. Doug was sitting by himself on the opposite end of the couch, still as a stone.

At last the paramedics maneuvered Beth onto a gurney they'd set up in the living room and took her outside. Doug followed, then came back a moment later.

"The laptop," he said to me, quietly. "I need it."

I shook my head. "Not a chance."

"Please," he said, leaning close enough that I felt the brush of his breath on my cheek. "It's important."

"Maybe," I said. "But you have much bigger problems now. And the first one is making sure Beth is all right."

"*Please.*"

I was about to turn him down a final time when an image of Cindy Morris popped into my head. I did some mental math. I thought about the irony of getting rid of the laptop after spending so much time chasing it. I weighed the headache of keeping it versus the one for giving it up. I was never very good at math. But in the end this answer came easily.

"OK," I said. Without a word I walked outside to my van. I opened the rear door, lifted the laptop out, and handed it to him.

"Knock yourself out," I said.

"Thanks," he said, relief in his eyes.

"Try not to screw things up this time," I said, then turned and walked back into the cabin.

A minute later, a tall, thin deputy walked in. I glanced over and saw that Anne was hovering in the kitchen, looking nervously in my direction.

"You who I think you are?" the deputy said, but not unkindly.

"Probably," I said.

"You know all these people here?"

"I do."

"Can you tell me what happened?"

"I can," I said. And I did.

WE WERE THERE ANOTHER two hours before the police finally allowed us to leave, and then only thanks to several phone calls back and forth between Burke and the sheriff and the local prosecutor. I knew instinctively it would not have done to explain the night's events only as a suicide attempt gone wrong. I had to tell them about Danny Reilly, too, and that opened the floodgates, as I knew it would. Eventually, just after 11 p.m., I drove back up the dirt road with Anne beside me and a sheriff's deputy behind us, making sure we got on our way safely. He made sure we were on our way safely all the way to the county line a full eight miles up the road, at which point I saw him in my rearview mirror abruptly pull over and turn around.

"You OK?" I said at last, more than anything to break the silence. She was in no condition to drive, and we'd agreed to deal with her car later.

"Yes," she said.

*Liar,* I said, to no one but myself.

Back at her parents' house, just before she got out of the van, I said, "What was the password?"

She turned. "Sorry?"

"The new password. On the laptop."

She paused.

I waited.

"Woodyfuckinghayes123," she said.

IT WAS AFTER MIDNIGHT when I got back on I-71 to head home. I felt the last of the night's adrenaline fade away, and a deadening fatigue begin to take hold. I rolled the car windows down and took a deep breath. I'd been through a lot, but I had so much more to do, including an expedition starting early tomorrow—today, I corrected myself—that would take all the energy I could muster. Up ahead was a Speedway gas station, and on the spur of the moment I pulled in beside a pump. I got out and swiped my credit card and started filling up. Ignoring the warning signs about the danger of cell phones and gasoline pump explosions, I took out my phone and looked up the last number I hoped to call that night.

Fielding answered on the second ring.

"It's Andy Hayes," I said. "I'm sorry to call so late."

"What do you need?"

His voice was clear and sharp. I couldn't tell if he was still working or sitting in his living room watching TV or lying on his side in bed where he'd been asleep. I'd noticed that Fielding was like that. Always on, even when he was off.

"Danny Reilly," I said.

"Still dead."

I took a deep breath, and told him as much as I knew. The line was silent when I finished, and the silence continued just long enough for me to wonder, almost, if he were still there. Finally, he said, "I'll need a statement."

"No problem," I said. "Anything else?"

But the connection had already been cut.

# 40

IT WAS THE KIND OF NIGHT I COULD HAVE used a week to recover from, but I hardly slept, and woke up not long after 6 a.m., after barely three hours of sleep. I got up, made coffee, then checked my phone. As I'd expected, there were three missed calls from Doug Freeley. I deleted the voicemails without listening to them, then took Hopalong out for a short walk down the block. There were a few other dog walkers out, some of whom I recognized, but I scarcely acknowledged their nods and greetings.

I made the call at 7 a.m., the earliest I knew I dared. Somewhat to my relief, Dorothy Cunningham picked up after two rings.

"Andy?" she said. "What's wrong?"

"I'm sorry to call so early," I said. "I need to talk to Burke again."

She hesitated. "He's still asleep after last night. Like you should be. Is there anything I can do?"

"I have a favor to ask. A big favor."

"What is it?"

"I need a ticket."

"Ticket?"

"To today's game."

I ARRIVED AT BURKE and Dorothy's house on a large corner lot in the Berwick neighborhood on the east side a couple of minutes after 8 o'clock. Burke greeted me at the door with a cup of coffee.

"You look like hell," he said.

"Nicest thing anybody's said to me all week."

"You could have asked me about this last night."

"I hadn't quite thought it through yet."

"So typical," he said.

"What?"

"Calling plays on the line of scrimmage. Just like the old days."

He led me into the kitchen, where Dorothy was filling a bowl with slices of brightly colored fruit. She beamed at me. "Breakfast in just a couple of minutes. Pancakes OK?"

"I can't stay for long," I said.

"You won't have to," she said. "Just long enough for a little groveling." But she was smiling as she said it.

Burke and I wandered into the living room. We went over last night's events.

He said, "I'm guessing those files are what the FBI is looking for."

"Something like that."

"American Financial Health Care. Do you know how much that case is worth? That's trial-of-the-century caliber. And I'm shut out because you're too much of a conflict of interest."

"I know," I said. "I'm sorry. It just kept escalating."

"Don't worry about it. What I don't know about that kind of white-collar crime could fill a couple volumes. But maybe you could do a better job of communicating in the future."

"Message received."

Dorothy called us to breakfast. I walked into their dining room, pulled my chair out from the table, and looked down at my plate. A ticket to that day's Michigan game stared back. I picked it up and slipped it into my wallet.

"Thank you," I said, looking at Dorothy.

"Don't thank me," she said brightly. "Thank Burke. It's his ticket."

"YOU'RE UP EARLY ON a Saturday," Roy said when I called him about an hour later.

I explained what I needed. There was silence on the other end.

"You sure about this?" he said after a moment.

"As sure as I'll ever be."

OF COURSE YOU DON'T pull up in front of Ohio Stadium on game day, even in a white van with the words "Church of the Holy Apostolic Fire" spread across both sides. Roy got me to Lane Avenue, on the northeast side of campus, but no farther because the street was blocked off. It was 12:45 when I got out of the van and stared at the sea of scarlet and gray before me, a mix of thousands of fans headed for the stadium and thousands more content to watch on the TVs set up at every other tailgate party.

"Thanks," I said, standing with the door open as Roy watched me curiously. Theresa had come along for the ride and was sitting in the back, staring at the scene. "I'll see you in an hour."

"You sure you know what you're doing?"

"Not really."

"Didn't think so."

"One hour," I said.

I was wearing sunglasses and my Clippers cap, and for the first few minutes they did the job. A lot of the people on the

234

outer edge of the scrum were born after I'd left the university. To them I was just another middle-aged Buckeye fan. It wasn't until I left Lane Avenue and skirted the first encampment of tailgate parties outside the stadium that I heard someone yell, "Woody! Woody Hayes!" I kept walking, but quickened my pace. The scene was the same everywhere: families and friends gathered in knots under scarlet-and-gray canopies, tables piled with picnic food, pregame activities on portable TVs. A few had rented their own portable bathrooms, also scarlet and gray. Alcohol was banned in these campus lots, but judging from the number of cans in Ohio State wraparound insulating holders, along with the elevated buzz of conversation, the prohibition might not have been universal. Off to the right I spied Fletcher's Band Wagon. It was still the biggest, gaudiest of them all. He wasn't there, I knew. He was already inside.

The shouts of "Woody" multiplied the closer I got to the stadium. Joining a line outside gate 18, I stood self-consciously, aware of how many people were starting to look in my direction. After a minute, a roundish guy with a goatee wearing a giant Buckeyes' jersey that draped far past his waist shouted over to me. "Hey, you're Woody Hayes, aren't you? What the hell you doing here?"

"Woody Fucking Hayes," growled one of his pals, an even heavier guy who seemed as if he'd had more than a few.

I knew ignoring them would be a mistake, so I waved and said, "How's it going?"

"How's it going?" the first guy said. "I'll tell you how it's going. Season on the *line*," he shouted. "*Big Ten championship at stake. And you get arrested? Fucking arrested?*" He was so angry he actually started laughing, but it was a bitter, caustic laugh, and I thought for a minute he was going to come at me. But at that moment a campus police officer, attracted by the man's raised voice, began to walk toward us, and at the same time the line inched forward.

"Ticket, please," the woman said when my time arrived. White-haired, in white slacks and an OSU sweater, she looked to be in her sixties or even seventies. Somebody's grandmother. She glanced at me, recorded my ticket with her handheld infrared scanner, then looked back at me. "You ought to be ashamed of yourself," she said.

I put the ticket back into my rear pocket, took a deep breath, and started walking through the concourse. Burke had a club seat on the other side of the stadium, a long walk but putting me close to Fletcher's suite. Keeping my head down, I stayed to the far right of the crowded interior and heard just a few catcalls.

Less than ten minutes later I arrived at the "3 Club" entrance. The sunlit field beckoned at the end of the shadowed concrete passageway. Thoughts of coliseums and gladiators rose up, got swatted down. Head up, I thought, and walked out into the stadium.

A scarlet-and-gray sea spread before and around me. More than 100,000 people. I'd forgotten what a glorious sight it was. I looked to my left and saw the upper deck display of the last names and numbers of Ohio State Heisman trophy winners. A bit farther to the right: a row commemorating each year of the university's seven national championships. I didn't need reminding it might have been eight but for me. I looked briefly to the far right, across the field, to the sign honoring my own namesake, Woody Hayes: "13 Big Ten Titles. 5 National Titles."

Several thoughts battled for my attention. Pride, at having once been part of such a tradition. Shame, at what I did to throw it all away. Disgust, at how Fletcher and others like him had sullied the sport.

It's possible I could have lingered over this contradictory moment all day long. Instead, I turned and started to climb. I had a long way to go.

"Jesus Christ," a voice said as I started walking up the steps, already favoring my left knee. "It's Woody Hayes."

"Loser!" a voice yelled.

"Traitor!"

"Woody *Fucking* Hayes!"

*I had been out of control at the time, I admit it. Luxury wardrobe. Kick-ass sound system in my apartment. Red Jeep Cherokee, brand new, loaded. Money flowing, not all of which—all right, not most of which—I could have told you where it came from. And the arrogance. The attitude. And the girls. Lots and lots of girls.*

Two railings, about ten steps. Talk about momentum.

"You son of a bitch!"

"Get out of here!"

"You suck!"

*Her name was Mary. Met her at a bar. Not the first, second, or even third time that kind of thing happened. To this day I don't remember actually being with her. It's hard anymore to recall her face, though I'm sure she was pretty. And probably starstruck. What I do remember is answering the door to my apartment one Sunday afternoon and seeing her standing there, and not recognizing her right away, and then hearing her say, eyes shining, "I'm pregnant."*

"Fuckup!"

"Loser!"

"Bastard!"

*Turns out she was pre-med and had three younger sisters who looked up to her and was on a full ride because her family was broke. A baby was out of the question. The abortion was $900, and she needed the money soon. And it quickly turned out that I'd misjudged her, as I usually did with women, because she wasn't going to take no for an answer. She wasn't going to walk away. She was going straight to the university, and beyond, if I didn't help her.*

Three more railings. Several steps. Left knee stiff as a board.

*It was Bobby Fletcher who stepped in. My old friend Bobby. Been to almost every one of my high school games. Quarry Chapel High out in Knox County. Personally introduced me to the Ohio State coach. Happy to loan me the money. More than a loan. "Consider it a gift." Just one little favor he had. Could I meet a friend of his. A guy he knew. Had a proposition for me.*

It was around this time that the pelting began from the empty plastic soda bottles and soft drink cups and wadded-up programs.

*So I met this guy, and there was a conversation, and some money changed hands, and quicker than I thought possible I had agreed to force some errors, to drop the ball, to narrow the spread. I helped shave points. Never threw a game, but polluted them, beyond question. Second Big Ten opponent of my senior year, Illinois, and three games after that. I never truly thought it was wrong. Just did it, you know, because I could, because I was Woody Fucking Hayes. Afterward, Bobby claimed he didn't know what the guy he'd introduced me to had really been up to. Thought he was just a fan. Like him.*

*The federal agents showed up at my door on November 17. Three days before the Michigan game. Up until that point, we were undefeated and ranked number one in the country. The best Ohio State team in a generation. Better than the '69 team, the one that would have been the all-time greatest except for the Michigan game they blew. Entire families, dynasties of Buckeye fans, had waited for such a season. I had been on the cover of* Sports Illustrated *just the week before. People bemoaned the possible impact of the so-called SI cover curse. But when it hit, it was not exactly what people had expected.*

You wouldn't think it, but plastic soda bottles sting quite a bit.

*I watched what turned out to be the last game of the season on a grainy TV inside the Franklin County Jail. For the record, Ohio State lost to Michigan 24–12, the same score as the 1969 game. Ironic, huh?*

I looked up and saw that I'd made it. There were eleven railings from the bottom of the Club seats to the level where the suites began, and I'd needed to hang on to every one of them. As I came to a halt I saw Fletcher emerge from the suite level of the concourse, staring at me. I walked up to him, faced him, then turned and gazed out at the stadium.

"No better sight in sports," I said.

"Jesus Christ," Fletcher said. "I can't believe you're here."

*It was a long road back. Prison time. Failed comeback attempt. Ill-advised marriages. Divorces. A couple bar fights. Finally, after a summer back on the farm in Knox County, slopping hogs under my uncle's stern direction, working fourteen hours a day in the sun, my head started to clear. I quietly finished my degree, mostly online. One day a former student manager for the football team, guy who'd been a senior my freshman year, amiable fellow named Burke, now a defense attorney in town, called to see if I could help him with a case. Needed someone to canvass witnesses in a tough neighborhood. He'd pay. I accepted. Rest is sort of history.*

I took a minute to catch my breath. It had been a long walk. And I was hurting. Right at the moment I wasn't sure I could bend my left knee.

I said, "Listen very carefully. I'll go slowly so you understand, and I won't use any big words. But I'm not going to repeat myself."

He stared at me, blankly.

"The tutoring services you've been providing are over. They're stopping today."

"What are you talking about?"

"You're going to sever all connections with Ohio State athletes. Is that clear? All connections."

"Listen—"

"And on top of that, Anne Cooper is walking away from this, and you're forgetting her name. She doesn't exist to you anymore. She never did."

"You're out of your mind," Fletcher said. "Absolutely out of your mind."

"It's possible," I said. "I've thought that for a long time. But the question right now is, have I made myself clear?"

"You left out 'Or else.' What are you going to do if I refuse?"

"I'm going to spill some ancient history."

"Statute of limitations ran out on that eons ago. You've got nothing."

"You're right."

"Of course I am."

"You're right that I have nothing to lose. I've been down as far as I could possibly go. Want to publicize the abortion? Be my guest. Want to remind people what a scumbag I was? Don't think that's a state secret."

"Get out of here, Andy. Just beat it."

"I kept your name out of it. The feds pushed me, pushed me hard. I could have been out a year earlier if I'd given you up. But I didn't. Because I was grateful for what you'd done for me. Pulled me out of East Bumfuck, Ohio, and got me to OSU. I knew I was the one who'd screwed up. I knew it was me who had to take the fall. Not you."

This time Fletcher didn't say anything.

"I know it's too late for anything legal to happen to you. But if I give you up now, you're persona non grata. They'll ban you from the stadium. No more tickets. No more tailgating. You'll be watching the game on a TV at home or in a bar like the other 99 percent."

"Get out," he said softly.

"It's over," I said. "Just remember that."

And with that I turned and walked onto the concourse. I knew I had to find an escalator. I'd climbed up, but I wasn't going to walk down.

IT TOOK ME ALMOST twenty minutes, surprise, to limp my way back to Lane Avenue, where Roy was sitting at the top of the street in his white van. He waved when he saw me approach. When I opened the door he whistled. I looked down. My clothes were spattered with mustard and ketchup.

"How did it go?" Roy said

"German Village," I replied. "And step on it."

But halfway there I remembered something. I turned to Theresa. "I think I owe you breakfast. Hungry?"

"It's lunchtime," she said.

"Waffles taste good any time of day," I said. "Especially the way I make them."

# 41

I SLEPT IN ON SUNDAY, THE FIRST TIME IN what felt like years, and even Hopalong left me alone until I was well and truly awake. My phone was full of messages from Doug Freeley, which I continued to ignore. After our walk, I strolled up to Cup o' Joe, and this time I made it through both pumpkin muffins and the entire sports section. I tried Anne's number twice, as I had tried it twice the afternoon before, but her voicemail picked up both times.

At 11:27 a.m. I pushed my key into the door of the judge's townhouse. "Laura?" I called.

She was at her desk at her computer, in her bathrobe, working as usual. Her hair was pulled back. She looked pretty.

"One minute," she said, without looking up.

I walked over to where she was sitting, leaned over and kissed her on the head.

"I said, one minute."

"I heard you," I said. I reached out and placed the key on the desk.

"What's this?"

"It's goodbye," I said.

She stopped typing and looked up at me. "What are you talking about?"

"You heard me."

During our time together I'd noticed it took a lot to get the judge's attention. For once, I had it.

"Don't be ridiculous," she said. "You don't know how good you've got it."

"Believe me. I know."

"Strings-free sex," she said, a little louder. "What more could a man want?"

"It's a good question. That's what I'm trying to figure out. That's why we have to stop."

"You're going to give me up? With your track record with women? Are you crazy?"

"Thanks a lot," I said.

"I'm sorry," she said. "I didn't mean it like that."

"Of course you did. It's OK. It's just time."

"Time?"

"It's time to move on. For both of us."

I WAS SCHEDULED TO take both boys in the afternoon, and while the exes tried to cancel in light of the Blue Jackets disaster the week before—and, to be fair, who could blame them?—I insisted, knowing I had the custody agreement on my side. We went to see a computer-animated movie in the Arena District downtown, a film whose plot escaped me ten minutes after we left the theater but which seemed to please the boys. I took them to Barley's in the Short North for barbecue afterward, and everybody was dropped off and home by seven o'clock. We even talked a little bit about homework on the ride to each of their houses. All in all, a successful outing.

The exes didn't exactly smile at me when I dropped the boys off, but they weren't openly hostile either.

MONDAY MORNING, I DIALED Cindy Morris's number right at eight o'clock. She picked up on the third ring, and from the noises in the background I could tell she wasn't at her office yet.

"Sorry to bother you so early," I said.

"I'm dropping my kids at school," she said. "What do you need?"

"I have something to tell you. Something important."

"I don't have my schedule in front of me. How about ten o'clock? At the office downtown."

I thought about this. I said, "How about, you tell me where the school is and I'll meet you there."

"What exactly do you have?" she said, impatiently. I heard a child's voice saying "Mommy" in the background.

"Something worth your time," I said. "Something about Doug Freeley."

The school was an elementary building in Hilliard, a suburb on the near west side of the city. Morris was parked in a black Chevy Blazer and typing furiously on her Blackberry when I pulled up two parking spaces away from her.

"This had better be good," she said, opening her door and getting out. "I don't let just anyone meet me at my kids' school."

"It's nice to see you, too," I said. Slowly, and carefully, I told her what I knew.

"You sure about this?" she said when I'd finished.

"Sure."

"Would have been nice to know earlier."

"Would have," I agreed.

"And remind me why we should ignore other things on the laptop? A bunch of English papers?"

"Professional courtesy?"

"We're not in the same profession."

"Honor among thieves?"

I might have been mistaken, but I thought I saw her smile.

After a moment she said, "This might involve some paperwork."

I shook my head. "I'd rather not get involved in paperwork."

"There's always paperwork," she said. "It's just a question of who the trail leads to."

I pulled out of the school parking lot before Morris did, and didn't bother to look in my mirror to see whether she stayed. She had all the cards now, and with one last exception, I was more than ready to wash my hands of Doug Freeley. I drove a couple of blocks until I reached the retail chaos of Rome-Hilliard Road, drove through two lights, then pulled into the parking lot at a Meijer grocery store. Engine running, I called Kevin Harding.

"I've been hearing some interesting stories about you," he said. "Were you really in Ohio Stadium on Saturday?"

"No comment."

He laughed. "You know there's about ten thousand pictures of you at the stadium floating around the Internet right now. People are saying it was the most tweeted event in Columbus history."

"I think that's the saddest thing I've ever heard," I said.

"Care to say anything about it?"

"Guess I'm glad Ohio State won, under the circumstances," I said. "Other than that, no."

"So why are you were calling? Maybe to explain why Doug Freeley blew me off Friday?"

"How often do you talk to Cindy Morris about American Financial Health Care?"

"I never talk to Cindy Morris. But I leave her a message almost every day."

"She never calls back?"

"Once," he said. "Told me to stop calling, that there was nothing new and she can't talk even if there were."

"Call again. Leave the exact same message you always do. Don't hint that you know something might be up, and for God's sake don't mention my name. When you're done, call the Hocking County Sheriff's Office and ask them about Freeley's wife."

"Whoa," Harding said. "What do you know?"

"I know enough to tell you exactly what I just said, and nothing more."

"Interesting," Harding said. "How about I return the favor. Tell you something you don't know."

"Like that would take a lot of effort."

"This one's good. Ted Hamilton."

"What about him?"

"Got arrested last night."

"For what?"

"Assaulted a girl in a bar. They had a disagreement about who was going home with who."

"Whom," I said.

"Screw you."

"That is interesting," I said. "Thanks."

"Should I expect to be hearing more about him?"

I thought about it. "I doubt it," I said. "Unless you're counting divorce filings."

# 42

I WENT TO BED EARLY MONDAY NIGHT with my phone turned off. I slept twelve hours.

I got up and checked my messages, hoping against hope for something from Anne. But all I had were three missed calls from Kevin Harding the night before and a text from Roy at seven o'clock that morning. *Nice work, champ*, it said.

It wasn't until I pulled the paper off the doorstep that I figured out what he was talking about.

The lead story that day was an article by Harding on the arrest of Doug and Beth Freeley of New Albany. Beth was facing state murder charges for the death of Danny Reilly. Doug was facing federal fraud and money-laundering charges for a variety of alleged improprieties at American Financial Health Care. I hadn't been sure anything about this case would surprise me anymore, but I found out I was wrong when I saw that the amount of misappropriated money could top $50 million. No wonder Special Agent Morris was so annoyed with me.

Next I flipped to the sports section. I saw the headline right away: "Three Players Suspended."

Ohio State's third-string quarterback, a running back, and an offensive lineman who started two games earlier this year have been declared ineligible for the Sugar Bowl after the university said all three had failed an English exam considered crucial to achieving a passing grade in a class normally taken by freshmen in need of remedial help.

I read carefully, my heart racing, but there was no mention of Anne. Fletcher had kept his mouth shut, for now.

Almost done, I said, heading to my bedroom to get dressed.

IT WAS JUST PAST 10:00 when I pulled into the Freeleys' driveway. I picked up that morning's copy of the *Dispatch* lying in its plastic bag at their front door and knocked loudly. It took two more attempts before the door opened and an unshaven Doug, wearing jeans and a faded Ohio State sweatshirt, stared at me in disbelief.

"What are you doing here?"

"Nice to see you too," I said. "We need to talk."

"Like hell we do. You're the last person in the world I want to see right now."

"Don't exaggerate. I'm sixth or seventh above the last person you want to talk to, easy."

"You need to leave."

"Not just yet," I said, and slowly but firmly pushed my way past him and went inside.

Everything looked the same in the Freeley home, but it all felt different. No other way to explain it. Loss and unhappiness and uncertainty clung to the furniture and the lamps and the designer paintings like a fog that had gradually crept inside and settled. The place felt cold, despite the comfortable temperature. Could it be that Beth, for all her issues and pretenses, for her long and enormous fabrication, had lent the house an actual feminine touch that was now gone, jerked away for good like the proverbial tablecloth from under the table settings?

"Did you get any of my messages?" Freeley demanded, following me inside.

"All of them," I said.

"Any reason you didn't return them?"

"I was busy."

"Busy like hell. You knew perfectly well when you gave me the laptop that Anne had changed the password. Fat lot of good it did me."

"Listen, Einstein," I said, turning toward him. "Try not to sound any stupider than you are."

"How dare you."

I held up my hand. I could tell he was deciding whether to say more. I waited until he lost his own internal argument. He looked like he'd aged ten years since our trip to the Hocking Hills. Not that I really cared.

I said, "This won't take long. The companies that American Financial worked with. Any rehab centers in the mix?"

"Rehab centers?"

"You know, addiction counseling. Places druggies go to get clean. Inpatient or out."

"I don't understand—"

"Just answer the question."

"Yes," he said, after a moment. "A couple. Why?"

"I'm going to tell you," I said. "Sit down and listen."

TOMMY WATKINS LOOKED ABOUT as happy to see me as the last time I'd stopped by the construction site. He came striding up to me with fire in his eyes after one of the laborers tracked him down for me.

"Hello again," I said, which was all I got out before he lunged at me and tried to land a pretty decent haymaker on my jaw. I stepped away in time, but just barely, and because he wasn't a guy used to throwing haymakers, he stumbled a bit and nearly lost his balance. I almost put out an arm to help him, but my knee made me think better of it. I took a couple of steps back.

"Son of a bitch," he gasped.

"You're probably right," I said. "So hear me out and then I'll be out of your hair for good."

"Fuck you."

Instead of responding, I held out an envelope. He refused to take it so I dropped it at his feet.

"Here's the deal," I said. "There's two things inside that. One is the name and phone number of a guy at Renewal Services over on the east side. It's a drug counseling place. Good reputation. Just call there and give them your name and your wife can sign up. For free. For as long as she needs. No questions asked." I paused. "They're expecting your call."

This had been easier to arrange than I'd anticipated when I first pulled up to Freeley's house. He'd been in the field long enough that he had some favors he could still call in under the table with companies he'd actually helped—ones that weren't lining up to sue him. The only inspiration he'd needed was my threat to finish the ruination of his family by going to the police about Pete and the video. I felt bad about playing that card, in part because it was a total bluff, but I didn't know any other way to cut the deal.

I continued. "Second thing, there's five hundred dollars in cash in there. Three hundred to make up for what you gave me for Reilly and two hundred for your troubles." Most of it was left over from Ted Hamilton. It was debatable whether he would want it back. I had plenty of uses for it, especially after bonding out Dave Brown, but that was beside the point.

We stood there then, neither of us speaking, stuck in a surreal standoff for what felt like an eternity but couldn't have been more than a few seconds. Just when I was starting to think I'd misjudged the operation, Watkins leaned over, took the envelope, folded it in half, and stuffed it into his back pocket.

"Get lost," he said, and turned and walked away.

It was good advice. I took it.

My next stop was Mary Miller's apartment. I'd like to say she looked relieved when I handed her the rest of the money I owed her. But she took it with a blank expression, almost as if she'd forgotten what it was for.

I was halfway out the door when she said, "Hey, Hayes."

I turned.

"You forgot something."

"What?"

It came flying down the hall in an arc. I reached out my right hand, old reflexes kicking in, and palmed it.

My Big Ten championship ring.

"Thanks," I said.

"Woody Fucking Hayes," she said, with a grin. "You're welcome."

# 43

THE COLUMBUS STATE PARKING GARAGE at Washington Avenue and Spring Street was almost full by the time I pulled in. I ended up nearly on the top level before I spied red tail lights and waited while a car whose license plate read "BUCK I 10" pulled out. I made a mental note to see if it were possible to determine how many other BUCK I plates there were in Ohio—at least 99, I was guessing. I walked down a level and then crossed over Spring using the pedestrian bridge, a structure sheathed in red interlocking metal tubes that also doubles as public art. "Passage," it was called, according to a plaque to my left as I reached the other side. Fair enough, I thought, reflecting on the events of the last few days.

I went down the three sets of stairs, walked along the sidewalk, then crossed under an archway into a large courtyard. There stood a towering white statue of Christopher Columbus, his left arm pointing the way it turned out I needed to go. I tipped the brim of my Clippers' cap in his direction, then headed over to the entrance to Nestor Hall. Inside, it took a few minutes of wandering around and overcoming my reluctance to ask directions before I ended up on the second floor. I found the classroom I was looking for, peeked to confirm I was right, checked my watch, then went back downstairs to a student lounge. I sat down, opened my Steve Jobs biography, and started to read. I had just under fifteen minutes to kill.

A chapter and a half later, I was interrupted by a figure looming over me.

"Illinois," a voice said.

I looked up. "I beg your pardon?"

A security guard was staring down at me. My age, with a few extra pounds, but not as pretty a smile.

"The Illinois game. Your junior year. You screwed up the spread. Cost me twenty bucks. Thanks a lot, Hayes."

I thought back to Danny Reilly in the alley. I'd screwed up the spread in other games. What was it with Illinois? And come to think of it, what was it with people in this town not letting go events that happened twenty years ago?

I closed the book and stood up. My extra inches of height trumped his spare tire. He took a step back, but the anger on his face remained.

"Mind if I ask what you're doing here?" he said.

"Yes," I said, and turned and headed to the stairs.

THE DOOR TO THE second-floor classroom was open. Anne was at the front of the room, her back to me, conferring with a young woman in a hijab and flowing yellow print dress. I stepped back and stood against the hallway wall and waited until the student, smiling broadly, holding a paper she'd obviously just gotten back from Professor Cooper, strode out of the room. I stepped inside. Anne still had her back to me, arranging papers on a desk.

I cleared my throat. "Excuse me," I said. "Is this New Beginnings 101?"

She turned, not recognizing my voice right away. She was wearing a dark skirt, beige blouse. and the same dark jacket she'd had on the day I met her.

"Andy," she said.

"I hope this isn't a bad time. I've been trying to reach you."

"I know."

"I just wanted to tell you . . . " I trailed off.

She didn't say anything.

"I owe you a new laptop," I said. "I don't think you'll be getting your old one back for a while. But I think everything's going to be all right. About the tutoring, I mean."

"I know," she said, almost sadly. She walked past me to the door and slowly closed it, pushing it until she heard the click of the latch. Then she turned to me.

"That's what you do, isn't that what you said? Make light of serious problems. Then fix them."

"Something like that."

She stepped a little closer. She brushed her hand along her cheek. She looked up at me. "Do you know how I got this?"

"I'm guessing you were stabbed."

"You're right. Do you know how?"

I shook my head.

"My husband tried to kill me. He was disturbed, mentally ill. And fortunately for me, a drunk—not that it seemed fortunate most days." She said this evenly, as if reciting the contents of a grocery list. "He stabbed me in the face and in the side, then stumbled over the coffee table chasing me. I locked myself in the bedroom and called police while he cut his wrists. He bled to death before I did."

I listened.

"Amelia was supposed to be home, but she'd gone over to a friend's at the last minute. Otherwise she might have been hurt too. Or worse."

I kept listening.

"He's the reason I'm so deeply in debt."

"How deep?"

"Five figures. *High* five figures. Who knew how much on-line porn cost? I do now. Found out afterward. In the hospital, actually."

I didn't say anything.

"If it's not screamingly obvious, I'm still trying to recover. I guess a sane person wouldn't run off to the Hocking Hills to have an affair with a man she scarcely knows."

"When you find a sane person," I said, "would you please introduce me? I'm still waiting to meet one."

"I'm sorry all this happened."

"Me too. But I think it's going to work out."

"I'm not so sure. I don't know if I can survive. Financially, I mean."

"That thing about me fixing things?" I said.

"Yes."

"I wish I could fix your debt for you. But I can't."

"I know."

"But I know someone who can."

"Who?"

"The lawyer I work for. Well, he can't either. But he knows people who can help. Consolidate your debt. Keep a roof over your head. Make it workable."

"Workable," she said. "That would be nice."

Unexpectedly, she tucked herself against my chest. I reached out and hugged her. We stood that way for a minute. Then separated.

She looked up at me. "Still interested after all that? Not too complicated for you?"

"You're talking to the king of complications. As you already know."

"You didn't answer my question."

Not knowing what else to do, I carefully and slowly bent my head down and kissed her. It was a good kiss. An overdue kiss, probably for both of us. A kiss that I didn't want to end.

"Yes," I said after a few moments. "Still interested."

ANNE HAD ANOTHER CLASS to teach, so we agreed to meet for a late lunch or an early dinner or maybe both. I felt as if nothing could spoil my mood, and I was right, even when I reached the first floor and spied my security guard pal stepping into the men's room. I was headed for the exit when I stopped, thought about something, then turned around.

He was at the urinal when I came in. I pulled a $20 bill out of my wallet, and keeping my eyes on the wall before me, reached over and dropped it at his feet.

"What the—" he started, turning in my direction. His eyes widened when he saw me.

"It was my senior year, Nimrod," I said. "Illinois, my senior year. Even the lamest Buckeye fan knows that."

I'm sorry. I couldn't help myself. I laughed all the way back to the garage.

# Acknowledgments

I'm grateful to Edith Ackerman and Gerry Hudson for reading early drafts of *Fourth Down and Out* and giving me the confidence to keep at it. Andrea Murray, one of the world's great editors, made numerous suggestions that improved the manuscript. I'm appreciative as always of the time she took and the effort she made.

Terry Myer of the Columbus Detective Agency and Rodney Armstrong of Securitas Inc. brought the lives of real-life private investigators into focus for me, for which I'm thankful. I also got help from Sgt. Rich Weiner at the Columbus Police Department, who was willing to act as a sounding board for my questions about police work. Mike Smith, Ohio Stadium building services coordinator, graciously provided a tour of Ohio Stadium that helped me visualize Andy's return to the Horseshoe after all those years.

I can't say enough about the continued support of everyone at Ohio University Press, and especially press director Gillian Berchowitz, who took a chance on the idea of Andy and made the series possible. Managing editor Nancy Basmajian shepherded the editing with finesse and good humor and pointed out several ways the book could be made better. I also appreciate the continuing work of interim sales and marketing director Jeff Kallet and am thrilled with the design that production manager Beth Pratt created. Finally, a tip of the hat to John Morris and his eagle copyediting eye; he made several saves that kept me from looking foolish. After all that help, any mistakes are mine and mine alone.

My children, Sarah, Emma, and Thomas, have been unflagging in their enthusiasm for this project and shameless in their roles as boosters. Their adventures across the city as young adults inspired me to illustrate what makes Columbus great. I owe a special thanks to Sarah, who helped solve a vexing character conundrum as we ran together one morning. Finally, it's no mystery how much I owe my wife, Pam, whose support of my writing now encompasses decades, including some treasured early years on the East Coast as we devoured Robert B. Parker's Spenser novels together. Thanks for helping this Andrew bring my Andy to life.

Andrew Welsh-Huggins, Columbus, Ohio

CPSIA information can be obtained at www.ICGtesting.com
Printed in the USA
BVOW04s1440120415

395705BV00005B/42/P